DEATH
OF A
DEACON

DEATH
OF A
DEACON
A MEG RYAN NOVEL

MICHAEL P. MCKEATING

XULON PRESS

Xulon Press
2301 Lucien Way #415
Maitland, FL 32751
407.339.4217
www.xulonpress.com

Printed in the United States of America.

ISBN-13: 978-1-54567-482-6

CHAPTER I

SISTER MOIRA FELT A HEADACHE COMING
on. She always got a headache when the conversation
turned to money. Especially the lack thereof.

The thin, wiry, grey-haired nun had a graceful
ease of movement which belied the fact that she was
approaching her seventh decade. When she entered the
convent and took a vow of poverty, she renounced own-
ership of money, but it seemed that she had always been
burdened with the duty of managing schools which
required money and lacked it.

She looked at the young man sitting across the
table from her. Rick Peters had been her assistant principal at St. Brendan's School for three years. He had
a school administrator's license from the state, and he
had a good recommendation from his previous school,
St. Malachy's in the inner-city, where he taught Math.
As assistant principal he was in charge of finances, discipline, buildings and grounds.

"But it's only early Spring," Sister Moira moaned. "How can we be having trouble making payroll already? We should be flush with Fall tuition money," she said.

Rick, tall and muscular with curly black hair, rolled his eyes and turned his palms up with a shrug of his broad shoulders.

"Tuition collections are slow," he observed. "Enrollment is down, the economy is tough, many of the parents are laid-off, others are on reduced hours. Money is tight for everyone, and we're last in line to get paid, because not paying us doesn't affect a person's credit rating."

"But what can we do?" she pleaded, to no one in particular. "Isn't there any way that we can speed up some of these tuition payments? Can we borrow on our line of credit?"

"The line of credit is maxed out. We need to go to our donors. We need to do some extraordinary fund-raising," Rick said. "I have some new ideas in that area. There's a new method of event fundraising that is being used very successfully by some colleges, but it'll take a little time to implement. I can't do it overnight. I'm afraid in the short run, we're going to have to ask Father Vince to advance us more money from the parish."

The frown on Sister Moira's face deepened, and a look of real pain appeared.

"Oh dear," she said "He won't like that. You know how tight he is with money. And we'll have to get through Deacon Tom first. You know how closely he watches the purse-strings. He'll have conniptions."

"Well I don't see any alternative," Rick replied. "This is Monday. Payroll is due Friday. The Parish Council meets Wednesday night. You'd better talk to Father Vince. You have a way of softening him up, and I'll talk to Deacon Tom and try to get him on board."

"Oh all right," Sister Moira said. "All I've ever wanted to do was teach fourth grade, and for years all I have done is deal with angry parents, raise money and worry about bills. I should have been a missionary."

"You know what you always tell me, Sister," Rick reminded her.

"And what is that?" she asked with a puzzled look.

"Offer it up for the poor souls in Purgatory," he said.

The brass plate on the dark mahogany door said "Director of Liturgy and Music Ministry." The door was open about halfway. It was in a suite of offices located in a long, narrow building connecting the Church with the Rectory. St. Brendan's consisted of a complex of buildings with the church, rectory and parish offices occupying one side of O'Connell Street, with a spacious parking lot behind the buildings. On the other side of the street St. Brendan's School occupied a two-story, brick and stone building in a U-Shape. It was constructed after World War II, and was still in reasonably good repair, although in need of a new boiler, upgraded windows, and roof repairs in spots.

Inside the office, Bruce Poole, the Director of Liturgy and Music, sat at a large, ornate, antique desk, strewn with open hymnals and sheets of music for various instruments. He was about thirty-five, somewhat flabby, with wavy blonde hair and smooth, clear skin. He had long-thin fingers as besuited an organist and keyboardist. He wore wire-rimmed glasses, of the half-lens variety, perched on the end of his nose.

Deacon Tom Flynn approached the open door. He was a man of about 55. He had close cropped grey hair cut in a buzz. His jaw was square, his neck was thick, and his build stocky. He might have been a Marine drill sergeant, or a retired linebacker. But in fact, he was far less healthy than he looked. He was a CPA who took early retirement from his accounting firm after a heart attack and triple coronary bypass surgery. After a period of recuperation and physical therapy, he decided to devote his remaining years to full-time church ministry. The Bishop assigned him to St. Brendan's as Pastoral Associate.

"Pastoral Associate" was one of those new titles in the Church which evade precise definition. The duties of the Pastoral Associate are whatever the pastor wants him to do, which is usually what the Pastor doesn't want to do. In this case the pastor, Father Vince, had assigned him to exercise general oversight of the budget, finance and personnel functions of the parish, including the school.

He rapped on the open door to catch Bruce's attention, and the younger man looked up with a look which conveyed something less than pleasure.

"Yes, what is it?" he demanded.

"It's about this request to hire the 'Fruits of the Spirit' choir to sing at the Easter Vigil Mass," Deacon Tom said.

Bruce immediately became defensive. "Yes, of course," he said. "I feel that it's very important to have a quality musical presence for the Vigil. 'Fruits of the Spirit' are well known for their contemporary praise and worship music. They are in great demand, but we can get them because the director is a friend of mine."

"That may be," Deacon Tom said, but their fee is nine hundred dollars. We already have a perfectly good choir here, which sings at the ten o'clock Mass every Sunday. What's wrong with them all of a sudden?"

"Their repertoire is limited, and they're not up to the quality of 'Fruits of the Spirit,'" Bruce huffed.

"That may or may not be so, but they are our parishioners, and they will sing at the Easter Vigil as they do every Sunday. I cannot approve an expenditure of nine hundred dollars for an outside choir," Deacon Tom said. "That's more than the usual collection at one Mass."

Bruce's face turned fire-engine red. "You're not the pastor," the fumed. You can't tell me what I can do."

"Yes I can," Deacon Tom said firmly. "Father Vince has delegated control of the budget and finances to me. I have to approve all extraordinary expenditures, and this is disapproved. And there's no use you appealing to father Vince. He's behind me one hundred percent on this."

Bruce banged his hand on the desk. "I won't accept this," he shouted.

"You'll have to," Deacon Tom said, and turned and walked away, leaving Bruce on the verge of apoplexy.

Bruce Poole was in the Music Room, rehearsing the students for the annual St. Patrick's Day Pageant, which was Father Vince's favorite event of the year. It was also the student's favorite event, because Father Vince always cried and gave them the next day off, after they capped a program of Irish classic songs with his all-time favorite, "The Rose of Tralee." It wasn't an easy piece to perform well, however, because it was in a high key, and required some sopranos to pull it off. It was best sung by boys whose voices had not yet changed.

The children had been at it a while and were getting restless, but Bruce was going over and over the lyrics with four fourth grade boys, Sean Dealy, Michael Riley, Joseph Plunkett and Tommy Malone, all sopranos, who were to do the *Rose of Tralee* for Father Vince.

"One more time boys," he said, "and then we'll break for today. on three. One, two, three:" He began to accompany them on the piano, and they sang:

The pale moon was rising above the green mountain,
The sun was declining beneath the blue sea;
When I strayed with my love to the pure crystal fountain,
That stands in the beautiful Vale of Tralee.

She was lovely and fair as the rose of the summer,
Yet 'twas not her beauty alone that won me;
Oh no, 'twas the truth in her eyes ever dawning,
That made me love Mary, the Rose of Tralee.

The cool shades of evening their mantle were spreading
And Mary all smiling sat listening to me;
The moon through the valley her pale rays were shining
When I won the heart of the Rose of Tralee.
She was lovely and fair as the rose of the summer,
Yet 'twas not her beauty alone that won me;
Oh no, 'twas the truth in her eyes ever dawning,
That made me love Mary, the Rose of Tralee.

Father Vince Doyle was seated at the table in the Rectory kitchen, drinking coffee and reading the sports page. The Bisons were in a slump, and their best starting pitcher was on the injured list. They were three games out of fourth place. Nothing to write home about.

Father Vince was tall and thin, with grey hair in a buzz, and a weathered face. He was born on a farm, one of eight children of second-generation Irish immigrants. He entered the seminary at 18, and was ordained at 25. He had served as a missionary in Bolivia for ten years and loved it. He was very disappointed when the Bishop had closed the Bolivian mission and called him home, but had dutifully obeyed. He was now in his thirty-seventh year as a priest. He was tough and practical, but with a good pastoral sense and empathy with the poor and weak.

"Excuse me, Father, may I join you?" Sister Moira said from the doorway of the kitchen.

"Sure. pull up a chair. You know where the coffee is," he said, glancing up from the sports page. "I don't know how we're going to get in the playoffs if the Mets keep calling our best players up. It's not like it'll do them any good anyway," he muttered, to no one in particular.

"Oh dear, they showed so much promise on opening day," she sympathized.

"Hmpf," he grunted.

"Father, I have to talk to you," she said.

He looked up from his paper. "Yes, Moira?" he said.

"I'm afraid it's rather serious. Rick Peters told me this morning that we can't make the school payroll on Friday. I hate to spring this on you, but I just found out. He tells me we're going to have to ask to borrow some money from the parish. He's gone to talk to Deacon Tom about it right now."

Father Vince looked puzzled and not too happy. "How can this be?" he asked. "Tom is keeping a close eye on the finances and he hasn't told me about any problems."

"Yes, I know," she said. I was surprised too. Rick says its a combination of the recession, declining enrollment, and slow tuition collections. Many of our parents are laid-off from their jobs or on reduced hours."

He knew that was all true, but he was still somewhat surprised that no one saw this crisis coming. He took a sip of coffee and thought about his limited options.

"We'll have to take this up at the Parish Council meeting Wednesday night, and we're all going to look somewhat silly. The trustees won't be happy about us springing this on them. There will be some blunt questions, I can tell you."

"I know. Oh dear, I'm so sorry, but there's nothing else we can do," she said.

"Yeah, well, your prayer group meets tomorrow night. You can pray to the Holy Spirit for the gift of discernment," he said.

"We will. A gift of money would come in handy too," she retorted. "We'll pray for that as well."

"It always worked for Mother Angelica," he shot back.

CHAPTER 2

DEACON TOM WAS SEATED AT HIS DESK IN the rectory, going over a draft of the parish financial report for the Parish Council meeting scheduled for Wednesday night. His blood pressure was still high from his confrontation with the organist. "Every church organist I ever knew was a pain in the butt," he thought. "They all think the world revolves around them and their concerns."

He heard a knock on the open door and looked up. It was Rick Peters, the Asst. Principal of St. Brendan's School. The last thing he wanted right now was another school problem. He put school principals and assistant principals in the same category as Church organists. Problem generators, with no clue about reality.

"Yes," he said.

"Deacon Tom, Sister Moira asked me to talk to you," the younger man began. "We find ourselves in the position where we have to ask for an emergency advance from the parish to make payroll on Friday."

"What?" the older man roared, ignoring the small voice that told him to calm down or he'd wind up back in the hospital. "How can this be? I thought your budget was balanced," he questioned.

"It was," Perry answered, "but this is a cash-flow problem. Tuition payments aren't coming in as projected due to the recession. Many of our parents are laid-off or on reduced hours. Utility bills are coming in higher than expected. Health insurance premiums have also gone up unexpectedly," he explained.

"How serious is it?" Deacon Tom asked.

"We have a cash shortfall of about $40,000," Perry replied.

Deacon Tom's eyebrows shot up. "That's not a small amount," he said. "How come you weren't minding the store? You should have noticed this much earlier."

"Of course I noticed all of the trends I've just mentioned, but I kept thinking they would straighten out. Tuition payments would come in. Maybe they still will. But meanwhile, we're out of cash."

Deacon Tom's eyes narrowed and a crease developed in his forehead. "I don't know if I fully accept this explanation. I'm going to want an audit of the books. I want you to bring me the school checkbook, the last six checking account statements, the accounts payable and receivable lists, the income statement and balance sheet."

The younger man's face turned beet-red. He looked like he was about to explode, but then thought better of it. "As you wish. You'll have them in an hour," he said. Then he turned and left.

Marty O'Connor sat forward in his desk chair, a frown on his ruddy, pock-marked face. He had the phone cradled on his left shoulder, and he brushed his right hand through his short-cropped, grey hair. He was stocky but fit, with a square jaw, deep blue eyes, and dimples in his cheeks which gave him a boyish look despite his sixty-two years. Marty was Director of Property Tax Assessment for the City, and was also President of the Parish Council at St. Brendan's. It was Monday afternoon. He had a Commissioner's meeting to prepare for, but he was on the phone with Father Vince Doyle, the pastor, who had just informed him that the Parish Council had to consider a request for an emergency loan to the parish school, which couldn't make payroll on Friday.

"But how does this happen, Father? How do we get blindsided like this? I thought they had a balanced budget. Couldn't they see this coming earlier?" he asked.

"Those are good questions, Marty," Father Vince replied. "They are the same questions I'm asking. They did have a balanced budget. I'm told that a number of the families are behind on their tuition payments, that utility bills were higher than normal, and that a number of the fundraising events, including the Silent Auction and the Night-at-the-Races didn't raise the amount that was budgeted."

"This is not going to sit well with the Parish Council, Father," Marty fretted. "You know that the Council is pretty much divided between supporters of the school, who are mostly parents of students, and those who, mostly without children or with grown children, would like to close the school and spend the money on adult programs. This fiasco will play right into their hands."

"I know, I know. Don't you think I've been thinking about that?" the priest answered.

"I know you have, Father," Marty answered. "But you and I are going to be on the hot seat Wednesday night, and we didn't create this problem," he replied. "You'd better pray for an angel to bail us out."

"I'm praying to St. Jude," the priest retorted.

"Why St. Jude?" Marty queried.

"Because he's the patron saint of impossible causes."

Bob Glinski, the parish custodian/maintenance man, rose from his knees and straightened up. He brushed the dust and soot from his work trousers. He had a wrench in his right hand and an oily rag in the left hand. He was tall, thin and hunch-backed, with thick, black hair. He had been in the Army for ten years, but was wounded in the war in Afghanistan and got a medical discharge. He was a cousin of one of Father Vince's classmates in the seminary, and it happened that the parish had been looking for someone with boiler and mechanical experience, so Father Vince had hired him, and his knowledge of all things mechanical made him worth his weight in gold.

He looked down at the controls of the school boiler. He knew the unit was on borrowed time. It needed either replacement, or at least a complete overhaul. He also knew that there was no money available for such an outlay, and that it was his job to coax another year or two out of it, one way or another. The current problem was a sticky shut-off valve on the gas feed. He had taken it apart, cleaned it and oiled it. He was sure it was good for another 3,000 miles, figuratively speaking, but he also knew the problem could recur at any moment, so would require constant watching.

He had removed the gas feed, which was a flexible aluminum hose, and cleaned it. He saw that the coupling was a little bit corroded, so he removed some of the corrosion with a little bit of sandpaper, greased it, and reattached it. He checked all the other connections and valves, paying particular attention to the pressure valves, and then began to pack up his tools and equipment.

He heard the hinges of a door squeaking, and he turned around to see one of the eighth grade students standing at the top of the short iron staircase leading down into the boiler-room. He recognized the boy as Sean Dealy, the son of a police officer. Sean was a bit of a loner. He neither fit in, nor got along, with most of the other eighth grade boys.

"What are you doing here, Sean? Bob asked. "You know the boiler room is off limits to students."

"I'm waiting for my Mom to pick me up," the boy said. "I saw that the door was open a crack, and I decided to investigate."

"Sean, your father is the cop, not you. I don't want you investigating. The boiler room is a dangerous place," Bob said. Then he added:

"Come on, let's go wait by the outside door, where your Mom can see you."

He escorted the boy out of the boiler room, down the hall to the side exit door of the school. He didn't hear the classroom door shut quietly further down the hall in the direction from which they had come.

Meg Ryan put the patrol car in gear, and pulled away from the curb, leaving the red Mustang and the somewhat testy motorist whom she had just written a speeding ticket behind her. She drove slowly south on McKinley Parkway toward McClellan Circle, in the center of which was the huge statue of the Civil War general astride his horse. McKinley Parkway was a good place to catch speeders, because it was a wide street with long distances between traffic signals. Meg's father had been a police officer, patrolling the same district for over twenty years. He had died suddenly of a heart attack when he was only 45 years old. Meg had grown up listening to his stories about working the streets, and she used the infused wisdom she had received from him every day. At that moment her personal cell-phone trilled. She pushed the lever under the steering wheel to activate the hands-free device.

"Hello," she said. "Meg," the voice on the other end said, "this is Marty O'Connor. Can you talk right now?" he asked.

"Yes," she said. "I'm on patrol, but I have no calls on the screen at the moment."

"I just got off the phone with Father Vince. He tells me that the school is going to come into the Parish Council meeting tomorrow night and ask for an emergency loan of $40,000 to meet payroll. They claim they are out of cash."

"What? How can they be?" she exclaimed.

"That's what I want to know," he said. "They have some explanations that seem plausible on the surface, but they don't add up in my mind."

"This isn't going to go over well, and you and I are going to be on the defensive," she said. Meg and Marty were part of the coalition within the Parish Council who were strong supporters of the school.

"I know, I know," he said. "I'm not comfortable with it, and I'm not happy with it, but Father Vince made it clear to me that he would like us to try and get it through. He has assigned Deacon Tom to do an investigation and figure out what is really going on, but meanwhile, we have no choice but to help them make payroll. And the less said about it publicly, the better. I wouldn't be good if the school parents found out that the school is insolvent."

"We can't really prevent that," she responded. "You know the Parish Council leaks like a sieve."

"Yes, I know, and the opponents of the school would be more than happy to spread the word," he noted. "Anyway, we need to try and get this passed. Can I count on your help?"

"All right. What do want me to do?" she asked.

"You speak to Grace O'Neill and Becky Nowak," he said. "They're school parents. They'll want to know how this happened. Stress to them that we need to fix the immediate crisis with as little debate as possible. Deacon Tom is investigating what the real cause of the problem is, and he will report to us at the next meeting."

At that moment the police radio in the patrol car began to crackle. "Cars in A District. "Violent domestic. 242 Coolidge. Cars responding?"

Meg picked up the microphone and pressed the key. "Adam 420 responding," she said into the mic.

"I'll speak to them, Marty. I've got to go now. I've got a call," she said.

Deacon Tom sat at his desk in the Rectory Annex, pouring over Income Statements, Accounts Receivable and Payable reports, and Cash Flow charts, which were spread before him. He was trying to follow the cash, and figure out why there was too little of it. The door of the office was ajar. He heard a knock and looked up. It was Lester Nestorius, a thin man of about sixty, with close-cropped grey hair, a thin mustache and a hawk-like nose. He was wearing a grey cardigan over a white shirt with a button-down collar. He was extremely near-sighted, and he wore drug-store cheaters, which perched on the end of his nose as he peered over the top of them. He anchored the far right wing of the parish spectrum. He was a *"Sede Vacantist,"* a member of an extremist group which takes the position that there hasn't been a legitimate Pope since St. Pius X, who died in 1914. They consider all Popes since them to be illegitimate. The main practical implication of this is that they consider the Second Vatican Council, and all of fourteen documents and constitutions, to be null and void. He was extremely critical and hyper-vigilant. He was, not to put too fine a point on it, a pain. Dealing with one of his pet peeves was the last thing that Deacon Tom wanted to get involved in at the moment.

"Yes, Lester? What is it?" Deacon Tom asked.

"It's about Bruce Poole, the organist."

"Yes, what about him," Deacon Tom asked rather testily.

"Some of the music he plays is disgraceful. He doesn't have proper respect for the liturgy. Some of the songs he chooses for Mass are irreverent, even syncretistic. And at Benediction, he always sings the Eucharistic hymns in English. You know it's tradition to sing "*Tantum Ergo*" and "*O Salutaris Hostia*" in Latin. People are complaining.

'Yeah, about three people. You and two of your cronies,' Deacon Tom thought to himself. But he also thought, 'the last thing I want to do at the moment is to get involved in a lengthy discussion of liturgical music.'

"Lester, I'm not a music critic. I can't sing 'My dog has fleas.' And I'm not the liturgical police, either. Right now I'm up to my ears in trying to balance the parish books, as you can see."

Lester's eyebrows shot up. "Why? Is there a problem? Are we in financial trouble?" he asked.

'You'd love that, wouldn't you?' Tom thought.

"No, we're not in trouble, he answered. "I'm just trying to make sense of these cash flow reports from the school before tomorrow night's parish council meeting."

Lester's eyebrows shot up. "Is the school having cash problems?" he demanded.

"Schools are always having cash problems," Tom answered. "It's a perennial problem. Now what can I do for you, Lester?"

"Well, nothing is more important that correct liturgy," Lester persisted. "That's why I am here, representing a number of parishioners. I think you need to do something about the abuses perpetrated by that prissy organist Father Vince hired."

'Prissy, is it?' Tom thought. 'Well he is, sort of, and that's what's really sticking in Nestor's craw. Now we're getting to the heart of the matter.'

"It's very important that the liturgy be done correctly, and that includes the liturgical music," Lester continued. "He thinks the Mass is entertainment and he is the entertainer. He's turning the Mass into a rock concert."

"Oh come on, that's a bit overstated, Lester. There's room for different kinds of music in the Mass," Tom said.

"No it's not overstated. This is a serious problem. People are upset. I'm putting you on notice. If something isn't done about it, people are going to start writing letters to the Bishop and to the press."

Tom saw that he'd better defuse the matter.

"Okay, I'll have a word with him, Lester. Now if you'll excuse me, I've got to get back to these reports to prepare for tomorrow night's meeting."

"Well, I hope you'll take this seriously. We'll be watching to see if there's any change," Lester warned ominously.

'You're always watching,' Tom thought. But he said, "Very well, I'll see to it, Lester."

CHAPTER 3

IT WAS 6:45 PM ON WEDNESDAY, AND members of the Parish Council were beginning to arrive for the regular monthly meeting. Judge Sadowski was the first to arrive, as usual. He was a retired City Court Judge in his seventies, who had been on the Parish Council for as long as anyone could remember. He was tall, slender built, but with a little paunch around the middle. He had wavy, white hair, thick bifocals with silver frames, angular face and brows creased with a permanent frown. He had been known for his crankiness when on the bench, and he was no different in Parish Council meetings.

Next to arrive was Grace O'Neill. She was an attractive, friendly woman with long, black hair parted in the middle. She was a law school graduate, admitted to the bar, who had quit her job when her first child, Bridget, was born. She had decided that motherhood was a higher calling than the law, and she threw herself into it with gusto. She now had three children in the parish elementary school, Bridget in fifth grade, Sean in third, and Siobhan in first. She took her seat at one corner of the table, at the opposite end from the judge.

Close on her heels, Becky Nowak entered. She was Grace's close friend and alter ego. Becky, a short woman with sandy hair usually combed back in a bun. She had two boys in the parish school, David in fifth grade and James in fourth.

Next came Jim Curran, an insurance underwriter in his fifties. His children were all grown and on their own, leaving he and his wife Paula with empty-nest syndrome. They both devoted a lot of time to volunteer work with the parish. Behind him came Joe Browne, a retired firefighter and widower with no children. He divided his time between the Tea Party and the parish, in that order. Lester Nestorius was next, bustling in with a quick step and plunking down next to the Judge. He nodded to Judge Sadowski and Jim Curran, and set down a thick folder.

Father Vince, Deacon Tom, Rick Peters, Sister Moira and Bruce Poole quickly filled up the rest of the room and took their places at the long table. Father Vince opened the meeting with his customary prayer to the Holy Spirit for the gifts of wisdom and discernment, and then turned the meeting over to Marty O'Connor, who began methodically leading the group through the agenda.

The meeting went relatively smoothly, with the Judge and Joe Browne keeping their crankiness to a moderate level, until it came to the "New Business" section of the agenda.

"We have a request from the school for an advance of $40,000 from the parish, which we are told is needed to meet payroll on Friday," Marty said.

It was as if Joshua had blown his trumpet. The walls of Jericho started coming down. All hell broke loose!

Lester Nestorius fired the first salvo. "Forty thousand dollars? How can they be forty thousand dollars in the hole? They're charging tuition of $3,000 a year! What's going on here?" he demanded.

"How can this happen?" Jim Curran demanded. "You told us the budget was balanced. How can you discover at the last minute that you can't meet payroll on Friday? Who's minding the store?"

"It's a cash flow problem," Rick Peters explained. "Tuition collection is running significantly behind.

Many parents are laid-off from their jobs, and have fallen behind in their payments."

"You have to make them pay," Joe Browne shouted. "There's no free lunch. If they don't pay, throw them out. Make an example of a couple of them. The rest will fall in line!"

"Oh dear, we can't do that," Sister Moira said. "This is our ministry. It's our mission. We are not only educating these children, we are handing on the faith to them.

What kind of example would that be? It's not all about money! This is a Catholic parish, not Walmart," she cried

"It may not be all about money," Judge Sadowski chimed in," but it can't operate without money. We have to pay our bills, or the utilities will be shut-off. We also have to pay not only the teachers salaries but their pension contributions, health insurance premiums, unemployment and Workers Comp insurance, etcetera. If we don't, the Bishop will shut us down. We can't print money, and we can't ignore it either."

"I don't buy this explanation at all. Somebody's been asleep at the switch," Joe Browne said, as he glared at Sister Moira and Rick Peters who were sitting next to each other. "I demand an audit of the school's books."

"I'm on that already," Deacon Tom announced. "I've collected the school checkbook, bank statements, and financial records, and I am conducting an internal audit. As you know, I'm a CPA, and I will present you with an audit of the schools books at the next meeting. But meanwhile, I really feel that we have no choice but to advance the school $40,000 out of our parish savings account to the school. We cannot miss a payroll. That would be front-page news, and it would be death to the school."

"It won't survive anyway. Better to die quickly than slowly," Joe Browne said.

"The school will survive! We cannot and will not let it close," Grace O'Neill shouted.

"And we won't allow it to miss payroll either," Becky Nowak added. "Our mission is to hand on the faith to the next generation, and we're going to do it. Without a school, we're not doing our mission, and we might as well not have a parish," she said.

"The children can go to public schools for free," Lester said. "It's the parents who have the primary responsibility to hand on the faith. Let them do it at home. They can do a better job of it than those artsy-fartsy teachers we have in our so-called Catholic school anyway," Lester said.

"Now Lester," let's not get personal," Fr. Vince said.

"Well, I think we've had enough discussion," Marty said. "Is there a motion?"

Meg Ryan picked up the cue. "I move that we approve an advance of $40,000 from parish savings to the school to be used to make payroll," she said.

"Second," Grace O'Neill and Becky Nowak shouted in unison.

"Moved and seconded. All in favor?" Marty asked.

"Aye," Meg, Grace, Becky, Deacon Tom, Sister Moira, Father Vince and Marty said.

"Opposed?" Marty asked.

"Nay," Jim Curran, Joe Browne, Judge Sadowski, and Bruce Poole said.

"The Ayes have it," Marty announced. "Deacon Tom is directed to transfer $40,000 from parish savings to the school payroll account.

The rest of the meeting went quickly, but ended with an uneasy tension in the air. The sharp division in the Parish Council between the pro-school faction and the anti-school faction was very apparent. This had been simmering for some time, but the sudden payroll crisis brought it out into the open.

Father Vince and Deacon Tom were hanging up their vestments in the sacristy after 8:00 Mass the next morning.

"Stormy meeting last night," Father Vince said. "I don't like these divisions in the parish. If we can't even agree on our mission, what's the point?"

"It's not new," Deacon Tom said. "It has ever been thus. Read St. Paul's First Letter to the Corinthians. Not more than ten years after the Ascension they were arguing between Paul's faction, Apollo's faction, Cephas' faction, etcetera. It's human nature. It's an effect of original sin."

"I know, I know. But it's very discouraging. I never really get used to it," Father Vince said.

"I'm going over to the school now discuss some questions I have about the financial records with Rick Peters," Deacon Tom said.

"There isn't anything wrong, is there?" Father Vince asked with a trembling voice.

"I don't know. I'm not jumping to any conclusions. I just have some questions, that's all."

As Deacon Tom was exiting the sacristy, Bruce Poole was descending from the choir loft.

"Tom, I'd like to revisit the subject of the Easter Vigil liturgy with you," Bruce said.

"Not now," Tom said, as he continued walking. "I told you we're not spending any money on a rock band."

Bruce's voice rose two octaves. "The 'Fruits of the Spirit' are not a rock band. They're a Contemporary Liturgical Music Ensemble. They're highly sought-after."

"Good. Then they don't need our business. Not a penny, Bruce," Tom said as he continued walking.

"I don't know who you think you are," Bruce screamed. "You going to get what's coming to you."

"Get in line," Tom responded.

Rick Peters was seated at his desk and Deacon Tom was standing beside him, looking over his shoulder.

"Rick, going over the P & L, the Total Tuition, Tuition Collected and Accounts Receivable don't seem to reconcile," Deacon Tom said.

Rick looked up sharply. "Are you accusing me of cooking the books?" he demanded.

"Not at all," Tom said. "I'm sure the answer is apparent. I know you're not an accountant and you're not totally familiar with this stuff. I'm sure it's all there. But I'm going to have to take these bank statements and cancelled checks and see if I can reconcile. The Parish Council expects a thorough report at the next meeting. You know that."

"You're not going to find anything. You're just wasting time and interfering with our operation."

"It has to be done, Rick. I have my marching orders, and the sooner I get at it the sooner I can get it done."

"If you don't trust me, maybe I should leave," Rick fumed.

"I didn't say I don't trust you. Do as you like, but I have to do what I've been directed to do," Deacon Tom said.

CHAPTER 4

THE NEXT DAY WAS FRIDAY. IT WAS A beautiful day. The sun was shining, the temperature was seventy degrees, and green leaves were sprouting on the trees. A perfect Spring day in the northeast. Grace O'Neill and Becky Nowak were in the school, sitting at a table near the door to the cafeteria. Every Friday morning they sat there selling gift cards for stores, restaurants and gas stations. The parish Home School Association got a commission on each card sold, and the proceeds were used to pay for sports uniforms and equipment for the parish school.

"We just got that resolution through by the skin of our teeth Wednesday night," Becky observed.

"Some of those old salts on the Parish Council are Neanderthals," Grace said. "I wanted to whack Joe Browne with a ruler."

"Sometimes people without children can be very selfish," Becky observed. "I'm sure if they had young children attending the school, the shoe would be on the other foot."

At that moment one of the cafeteria workers approached the table and spoke to the two women. "Do you girls smell anything funny," she asked.

They both wrinkled their noses and sniffed. "To tell you the truth, it smells like gas," Grace said. "I thought it was coming from the stove."

"No it isn't," the cafeteria worker said. "But it does smell like gas, and it's getting stronger." Grace and Becky looked at each other. "What do you think?" Becky asked.

"I'm going to go to the office and tell Sister Moira," Grace said.

At that moment, Sister Moira came down the staircase next to the cafeteria. "Do you smell gas?" she said to the three women.

"Yes, we do. I was just coming to tell you," Grace said.

"We smelled it all the way upstairs in the office. Is it coming from the stove?"

No, it isn't," the cafeteria lady said. "It seems to be coming from the boiler room."

"Oh dear. Maybe I should go down there and investigate?" Sister Moira said, without much conviction.

"I wouldn't open that door," Grace said. "Call the Fire Department. Let them do it. That's what they get paid for."

"I guess you're right," she said.

"Nine-one-one, fire and police, what is your emergency," the impersonal voice barked through the phone.

"This is Sister Moira, principal of St. Brendan's School, 525 O'Connell Street. We have a strong smell of gas in the school."

"Where is the odor coming from?" the dispatcher asked.

"It seems to be coming from the boiler room," Sister Moira answered.

"Are there any children in the school?"

"Yes, school is in session. There are 320 students here."

"Pull the fire alarm and get them out and away from the building as quickly as possible. We're on the way."

Sister Moira hung up the phone and walked out into the hall.

"Well?" Grace asked.

35

"They said to get everyone out immediately," sister Moira said as she walked over to the wall and pulled the nearest fire alarm. A bell started clanging, a horn started bellowing, and teachers and students started pouring out of the classrooms.

The Fire Department radio sprang to life with three high-pitched tones.

"Engine Four, St. Brendan's School, 525 O'Connell Street, smell of gas in the school. Evacuation in progress. Time of alarm, 9:25 AM," the dispatcher barked over the radio.

Within a minute there was a response. "Engine Four responding to St. Brendan's," the voice came back, competing with the siren in the background.

Meg Ryan was driving down South Park Avenue in her police car, sipping the cappuccino she had just picked up at the Starbuck's drive-through. It was a slow day, and she was fighting boredom. She was daydreaming about Joe Curry, a detective in her district whom she had recently started dating. It seemed like he might be a keeper. He didn't seem to be like most cops she had dated--heavy drinkers and philanderers, with vocabularies which seemed to contain a lot of Anglo-Saxon four-letter words used as verbs, adverbs and adjectives at the same time. He was polite, courteous, and could talk about other things besides booze, sex and sports. Seemed too good to be true.

She was also turning over and over in her head the events of the night before. She was a graduate of St. Brendan's herself. It was an Irish working class neighborhood. Police officers, firefighters and civil servants lived on almost every block. She had wandered away from the faith in college and through several failed relationships, but about five years ago she had experienced a "reversion" on a weekend retreat for young singles, and had deepened her involvement in the Church ever since. Spectacles of bickering and division like the previous evening's parish council meeting deeply disturbed her. She found herself musing about the nature of the Church, as, in Pope Francis' words: "A hospital for sinners, not a hotel for saints." Suddenly the police radio in her car came alive.

"Cars in A District. Smell of natural gas escaping at St. Brendan's School, 525 O'Connell. Building being evacuated. Fire is on the way."

Meg put down the cappuccino and activated the siren and overhead lights. "Adam four-twenty responding to St. Brendan's," she called over the radio. She swung the police car around and cut down a series of side streets as the quickest way to get from South Park Avenue to O'Connell Avenue. The police radio crackled again. "Cars responding to St. Brendan's, be advised the children are evacuating to the Church. Fire Department and EMS responding." She turned onto O'Connell Avenue and floored the accelerator. Cars pulled over to the curb to get out of her way. As she rounded Griffin Circle she could see the high spire of St. Brendan's Church five blocks ahead. She glanced in her rear-view mirror and noticed a fire engine close behind her. She pulled into the driveway of St. Brendan's and jumped out of the patrol car. Leaving it with the engine running and the overhead lights on, she ran into the Church.

St. Brendan's was an old Church that had been modernized on the interior, with the pews arranged in a semi-circle, the altar and sanctuary in the middle. The children were all sitting in the pews, arranged according to their grades just as they would be for a school Mass, with their teachers on the end of the pews. At first, the scene appeared calm, but noisy. Sister Moira was in the podium, giving orders over the P.A. System, and trying to maintain order. She instructed the teachers to pull out their cell phones and class lists, which they are required to carry with them on an evacuation, and to start calling parents to come and pick their children up. Sister Moira knew intuitively they would not be returning to the school that day. Suddenly, a child in the second row fainted. The girl next to her screamed. Other children began crying. A boy of about eight started running toward the lavatory, and didn't quite make it. He heaved his breakfast on the marble floor. More children started complaining of feeling sick. The two EMT's who had arrived from EMS were getting overwhelmed already, moving from child to child. Meg looked around, wondering where the firefighters from Engine Four were. She could use a little help. Then she realized that they had gone to the school across the street, and were trying to deal with the gas leak.

She pulled the portable radio from her gunbelt and depressed the key. "Adam four-twenty to Radio. We need more manpower here at St. Brendan's Church. We've got kids down all over the place. We need more ambulances, EMT's. We need Fire Rescue."

The police radio became a cacophony of sound. Before the police dispatcher could even speak, car after car called that they were responding. Meg knew that a number of police officers on duty had children in St. Brendan's, and they were going to be responding from wherever they were, with or without permission. Suddenly she heard a deep baritone shout over the police radio: "C-One responding." The Commissioner of Police himself was on the way. Things were going to get dicey.

Meg helped a teacher move some sick children into the Narthex of the Church and line them up on the carpeted floor. More police officers were arriving. One of them was Kathy Meegan, a close friend of Meg's, who had a daughter in fifth grade in the school. Lieutenant Matt Donovan came running in. He had a son in eighth grade. More EMTs arrived, and began creating triage areas, ranking the children according to severity of symptoms. An EMT appeared at her side, and began assessing a child.

"They just all started going down at once," she said.

"That's how carbon monoxide hits you," he said. "Some of this may also be mass hysteria, but at this time we can't tell what part, so we have to treat it all the same."

"We need more help," she pleaded.

"The SMART Team is on the way," he said.

"What is the SMART Team?" she demanded with a puzzled look.

"Specialized Medical Assistance Response Team. A special disaster response team from the County Medical Center, with doctors and nurses. They'll be here any minute."

As Meg had turned left into the Church driveway, Engine 4 turned right into the school parking lot. The firefighters jumped off the engine and approached the school door. The Lieutenant, wearing a white shirt with a single gold bar on each collar, got out of the cab with a carbon monoxide detector in his right hand.

"Don't go in yet," he ordered the three firefighters in blue uniforms.

He approached the door with the carbon monoxide detector in his hand, switched it on, and slowly entered the building. He moved through the corridor toward the main hall of the school. The carbon monoxide detector was clicking, and the clicking gradually became more rapid. He looked at the gauge, which displayed the carbon monoxide level in parts per million. The needle edged from two hundred up to four hundred, and went from the yellow-shaded area to a red-shaded area. He reached the main hallway and turned right toward the cafeteria. Beyond the cafeteria was the door to the boiler room, which was slightly ajar. As he moved toward the cafeteria, the needle jumped from four to eight hundred, and the clicking grew even more rapid. When he reached the door of the cafeteria he looked down at the gauge again. The needle was well into the red territory, and registered 1,600 parts per million! He turned on his heels and moved toward the exit as rapidly as possible, taking care not to run, because he didn't want to increase his respiration and inhale more carbon monoxide than he already had.

He exited the building and yelled to the other three firefighters: "CO is 1,600 parts per million, well above the danger level. Anybody who was near that cafeteria should be exhibiting symptoms of CO poisoning!"

He jumped in the cab of the engine and grabbed the radio microphone. "Engine Four to Radio: Balance of the assignment to St. Brendan's. Extremely high CO levels in the school. All units respond with air packs!"

Back at the Church, the SMART team had arrived from the County Medical Center. Four EMS ambulances were also lined up in the driveway. The first of them was backed up to the entrance of the Narthex, with its rear door opened. A young Emergency Room doctor was taking charge of the operation and bringing some order to the chaos. He was about thirty, short, with curly black hair, dark complexion, and a calm, self-assured manner which belied his age. He was clearly used to being in charge, and to being obeyed. He had organized the children on the floor of the Narthex according to the perceived seriousness of their symptoms. They were laying on colored, plastic tarps--yellow, orange and red, with red indicating the most serious cases. The children had masks on their noses, connected by plastic hoses to oxygen tanks. They also had an instrument that looked like a plastic clothespin on their index fingers, measuring the blood oxygen.

Parents were beginning to pour into the Narthex, all of them wearing anxious looks on their faces, and some of them were nearly hysterical. Father Vince arrived and was moving from child to child, parent to parent, offering comfort and solace. Meg was helping Kathy Meegan, a fellow officer on-duty, comfort her daughter

Rosemary, a fifth-grader. Rosemary had asthma, and was having obvious difficulty with shortness of breath.

Father Vince approached Meg. "Have you seen Deacon Tom?" he asked her. "No, come to think of it, I haven't seen him since I arrived," Meg said.

Father Vince frowned, "That's unusual," he said. "He was here for morning Mass, and he didn't say he was going anywhere. But I can't imagine he hasn't heard all this commotion and come in here before now," he said.

Meanwhile, the young trauma doctor came up to Rosemary Meegan and glanced at the blood ox monitor on her finger. It read 90. "Hi, I'm Doctor Aquino," he introduced himself. "Has this child any history of respiratory difficulties?"

"Yes," Kathy said. "She has asthma." The doctor frowned. "Nurse," he barked, and one of the nurses came over to Rosemary. "Stay with this girl." If the blood ox doesn't rise in five minutes, or if it falls below 88, come and get me immediately." He moved on the next child. Meg glanced at Kathy, and saw her eyes begin to tear up. She moved over and squeezed Kathy's hand. "She'll be all right," Meg said, conveying more confidence than she had.

Across the street in the school, Battalion Chief O'Boyle and Lieutenant Greco, who was the first fire officer on the scene, entered the school, wearing full turnout gear and air packs. They moved slowly toward the cafeteria and boiler room, with the Lieutenant still holding his carbon monoxide detector.

First they entered the kitchen of the cafeteria, to check the large commercial stove and oven as potential sources of carbon monoxide. They quickly ruled out those sources, however, both because there was no apparent malfunction in either appliance, and because the CO level was not as high inside the kitchen as it was outside in the hall.

They exited the kitchen, and moved toward the boiler room door. As they entered the boiler room, the CO detector went crazy. They headed down the short metal staircase leading to the boiler. The Chief immediately noticed that the pipe bringing the gas supply into the boiler was disconnected, allowing gas to escape into the air of the surrounding room. He also noticed something else. A man was laying on the floor next to the boiler. He was crumpled in an unnatural shape, surrounded by a pool of blood, face-down, with a large dent in the back of his head.

He was quite obviously dead. The Chief approached the boiler, shut off the valve on the gas supply, and the two firefighters beat a hasty retreat.

CHAPTER 5

MEG WAS IN THE NARTHEX OF THE Church when she noticed the Fire Chief enter and hurriedly walk up to Lieutenant Donovan and begin speaking to him. Lt. Donovan's face suddenly looked grave -- surprised and alarmed at the same time. He took out his cell phone and made a call. As soon as he finished the call he motioned to Meg to follow him. They both exited the side door of the Church into the driveway. As soon as they cleared the door, he turned to her and said: "We've got a crime-scene across the street. Get some crime-scene tape out of your patrol car, some evidence bags, gloves and markers, and follow me.

"What kind of a crime scene," she asked.

"Homicide," he answered grimly.

Meg went to her patrol car and removed the crime-scene kit from the trunk. She trotted to catch up with the Lieutenant as he was crossing the street. At that moment she heard the portable radio on her belt crackle.

"Car 26 and CSI 310 respond to St. Brendan's School, 525 O'Connell Street, in the basement boiler room."

At that time, the Battalion Chief and two fire-fighters were placing a heavy-duty exhaust fan in front of the door.

"It's not safe to enter yet," he said. "The CO level is very high. We have to pull some of it out with this exhaust fan first. I've also got two men in air-packs opening all the windows."

It seemed like eons until the Chief gave the all-clear to enter, but it was actually about five minutes. During that time a Homicide car and the CSI team rolled up. Finally, the Chief exited with a CO detector in his hand and pronounced the building safe.

The officers entered the school, turned right, walked down the hall to the boiler room, and descended the stairs. There on the floor next to the boiler, in a pool of blood already partly congealed, was Deacon Tom. He was lying right next to the boiler, face-down, with already-clotting blood caked in his hair and on his black clerical shirt.

The CSI detectives began donning their white suits. Sgt. Keane, one of the homicide detectives, bent over the body and began to examine it, searching carefully for other marks and wounds besides the obvious dent in the back of the head. He noted a bruise on the neck, and also a tear on the back of his shirt. He turned the corpse over on its back. Deacon Tom's eyes were open with that vacant stare of the dead. His mouth was also open, and there was a look of shock and surprise on his face.

Meg shuddered. She was trying very hard to control herself in front of the Lieutenant and the firefighters, but it was a losing battle. She had grown very fond of Deacon Tom. He had a gruff, businesslike exterior, but was actually he was a Teddy Bear on the inside. He always had a soft spot for anyone who was down and out or in need in any way. Over the years, he had been a sympathetic ear for her many times as she went through the break up of romances, as well as the death of her mother two years before. Conflicting emotions began to well up within her: grief, sadness, and overwhelming anger at whoever could have done this.

She was also frustrated because she knew she would not be able to play any significant part in the investigation. Her ambition was to be a detective, and she was on the civil service promotional list for detective, but had not been called yet. She was still a lowly P.O., and as such, she would not be allowed to play any major part in the murder investigation that would follow. She fervently hoped that the perpetrator would turn out to be some random tramp acting on a base motive. But she knew that, statistically, most murder victims are killed by someone they know; and if Deacon Tom was killed by someone he knew, it was also probably someone that she knew.

Sgt. Amico went through Deacon Tom's pockets, emptying the contents and putting the item in plastic evidence bags. There was nothing unusual. Some change, a few dollars in currency, a wallet with ID and credit cards, a ring of keys, a rosary and a small notebook.

At that moment the Medical Examiner arrived. He was dressed in the regulation white crime scene jumpsuit, used by the CSI folks to prevent contaminating themselves or the crime scene. He walked up to Lt. Donovan and introduced himself. "Dr. Sanjay Patel," he said. He was an East Indian, tall and dark with straight black hair. He turned his attention to the body.

"When was he found?" he asked.

"About a half hour ago," Lt. Donovan answered. There was a carbon monoxide leak at about 9:00 this morning. The school was evacuated to the church across the street. The firemen found him, but we couldn't get in until they made the building safe by pulling all the gas out with exhaust fans."

Dr. Patel knelt down and examined the body. He rolled it over and noted the discoloration of the skin and the purple lips. "This is a very nasty gash on the back of his head, but I don't think it killed him," he said. "Right now, it looks to me like asphyxiation, but I'll give you an official cause of death after I complete the autopsy."

In the narthex of the Church, the emergency medical personnel were getting some organization and control around the treatment of the children suffering from carbon monoxide inhalation. Most were responding well to the oxygen they had been given. Some had already been taken off the oxygen and were sitting with their parents. But the ones on the red plastic tarps were still the focus of close scrutiny.

Rosemary Meegan was still laying on a gurney with the blood-ox gauge on her finger, her mother and a nurse at her side. The young ER doctor was working his way back to her. As he approached, the nurse looked up at him and their eyes met. The look on her face told him what he needed to know. He looked at the blood-ox gauge. It read 88. He looked at Rosemary's mother and said: "I'm afraid we're going to have to take her to the hospital. Her blood-oxygen level is not responding as it should, and since she's asthmatic, we just can't take any chances. "

Kathy's eyes filled with tears and she began to tremble. She nodded her head in recognition. The doctor motioned to two EMT's standing nearby. "We have to transfer this one to Children's Hospital, Code Three," he said. They began wheeling Rosemary's gurney to a waiting ambulance. The doctor took Kathy by the hand. "You can ride shotgun in the ambulance," he said. We can better get her stabilized at Children's, where they have the facilities. She'll be all right," he assured her, with a confidence he didn't feel. The EMT wheeled Rosemary to the ambulance and loaded her into the back. Another EMT helped Kathy into the front passenger seat, and then hopped in the back with Rosemary, and the ambulance roared off, lights flashing, siren blaring.

Across the street at the school, the Medical Examiner's staff were loading the body of Deacon Tom into a hearse, to be taken to the morgue at the County Medical Center, where an autopsy would be performed later. Inspector Flanagan, the A District Chief, had arrived, and was discussing procedure with the lieutenant and Sgt. Keane. Flanagan held the highest civil service rank in the department. He had 25 years on the job, and was Chief of one of the five districts in the city. He was over six feet tall, lanky, with curly white hair, blue eyes and a square jaw. He was well liked in the department, although he was a no-nonsense supervisor who insisted on discipline. He suddenly called Meg over to where he was talking with the other two superior officers.

"You knew the deceased, didn't you, Meg?" he asked.

"Yes, sir. I'm a member of this parish and I'm on the parish council. I knew him pretty well, and I was very fond of him. Everyone was."

"Apparently not everyone," Flanagan thought, but he let it pass without comment. "Do you also know his wife?" the Inspector asked.

Meg sensed where this was going, and she wasn't happy with it, but there was no way out. "Yes, I know her. Her name is Sheila. She's a very nice lady," Meg said.

"Well, I have to go and break the news to her, and I'd better do it immediately before it gets to her on the grapevine. I'd like you to come with me."

That was the last thing that Meg wanted to do, but she knew that she couldn't refuse. "Of course, Inspector," she said. "Do you want me to drive?" "Yes," he said.

Meg drove the police car, with the Inspector as passenger, down tree-lined side streets dotted with brick and clapboard style Cape Cod bungalows. She turned onto Wicklow Street and stopped in front of a brick, ranch-style home with an attached garage, manicured lawn, and a border of rose bushes across the front. "This is Deacon Tom's house," she said to the inspector. "His wife's name is Sheila." The Inspector glanced at her. "This is part of a policeman's job," he said, "but in case you're wondering, you never get used to it."

They walked up the driveway to the front door and rang the bell. The door was opened by a woman in her mid-fifties with salt-and-pepper hair pulled back in a bun.

"Why Meg, how nice to see you," the woman said. "Won't you come in?" Meg and the Inspector stepped into the foyer, which led right into the living room. They stepped into the living room and Meg said: "Sheila, this is Inspector Flanagan."

"Won't you sit down please," Sheila said with a puzzled look on her face. "What brings you here?"

Meg looked at the inspector who said, "Mrs. Flynn, I'm afraid there's no way to sugar-coat this. You husband is deceased."

She began to tremble and her eyes filled with tears. Meg instinctively moved to the couch and put her arm around Mrs. Flynn.

"Did he have another heart attack?" she whispered.

"No. I'm afraid it looks very much like foul play," the Inspector replied.

Her eyes widened and she gaped at him with open mouth. "Oh no, surely not," she said.

"I'm afraid so. There will have to be an investigation. You will be contacted by detectives. I'm very sorry for your loss, and sorry to trouble you with all of this, but I'm sure you will understand that we have to get to the bottom of what happened to him."

She was sobbing softly, twisting a tissue around her fingers. Her shoulders were shaking.

"I know this is hard to process," the Inspector said. "We will need to take a statement from you, but not now. Is there anyone who can stay with you tonight?"

"My daughter lives a few blocks away, on Seneca Street, with her husband," she said. "I think you should call her and ask her to come over," the Inspector said.

A half hour later, Mrs. Flynn's daughter had arrived and settled in to spend the night, and the Inspector and Meg took their leave, making arrangements that someone would call on her the next day.

Back in the patrol car, the Inspector said to Meg, "You're on the list for Detective, aren't you?"

"Yes, sir," she answered. "I'm fourth out," she said.

"You'll be made soon then. I'm going to detail you as an Acting Detective to work on this case. With your knowledge of the parish and all of the players, you can be very helpful in taking statements, as well as supplying background information on the cast of characters."

Meg was thrilled to get a shot at being a detective, but at the same time her emotions were ambivalent. She knew she would have to be very professional and maintain objectivity when interviewing people who were all friends, in some cases close friends.

"Thank you, sir," she said. "I appreciate the confidence. Do you really think it was somebody connected with the parish who did this?"

"Meg, you know as well as I do that most people waste a lot of time and energy worrying about being attacked by a stranger, when the statistics are overwhelming that homicide victims are killed by someone they knew, usually knew well."

"Yes I know," she said. "I'm just having a hard time wrapping my mind around it."

"Good," the Inspector said. "I'll assign you to work with Joe Curry. You know him don't you?" the Inspector asked.

"Yes, sir, I do," she said, trying to keep any hint of emotion out of her voice.

"That's all right then. He's a good detective. You and he will have to take statements from everybody who knew the deceased. That's going to be dozens of people, almost all members of the parish. So your presence might break the ice and make the interviews go smoother."

"I'll do my best, sir, and thank you for the chance," she said.

"I'm sure you'll do a good job," Meg, he said. "I knew your father, and you're following in his footsteps."

CHAPTER 6

THE NEXT MORNING MEG REPORTED TO the Precinct at 8:00 a.m. wearing a grey pants suit, with a belt around her waist carrying a Glock .9mm, a pair of handcuffs and some pepper spray. She walked into the Squad Room and poured herself a cup of coffee, thick as mud, as usual. The room, painted in drab green and filled with wooden chairs and tables, Spartan but sturdy, made by the WPA during the Depression, and sold to every municipality in the country. The room began to fill up with detectives, awaiting their assignments.

Inspector Flanagan entered, and everybody quieted down. He began the briefing. "The priority for today is the murder yesterday of the Deacon at St. Brendan's, a man named Thomas Flynn. He was married, wife named Sheila, adult children out of the nest. Appears to have been popular, no known enemies at this time. We also have no suspect at this time. We have to interview everybody who knew him. It seems like that will be a long list. Fellow clergy, employees of the parish, school parents, and members of the parish. I've detailed Meg Ryan as an Acting Detective to work on this case, because she's a member of the parish council, and knows all the players. She will be very valuable in sorting the wheat from the chaff, and also in spotting who's telling the truth, who's holding back, and who's blowing smoke at us," he said. "Meg," he continued, "you'll be working with Joe Curry. "I want you to start by interviewing everybody who worked in the church, including the pastor."

"Yes, sir" Meg answered.

Joe nodded in assent. "All right, get going," the Inspector said. He proceeded to give out assignment to the rest of the detectives, as Meg and Joe picked up their coffees and headed for the door. As they left, they took a set of keys from one of the hooks on the wall, and headed for a black unmarked Crown Vic in the parking lot. As they got into the car, with Joe behind the wheel, he looked at her, and she felt her neck begin to redden. "Damn, why do I always get flustered and blush," she thought.

He grinned at her and said, "Well, this is your turf. You know the players, where do we begin?"

"Well, I guess we might as well begin with Father Vince," she said.

"Is there any background I need to know?" he asked as they drove the short distance to the Church.

"There may be," she answered, and proceeded to brief him on the controversy in the parish council over the school cash-flow problem.

"Mmn," he said. "Think somebody was cooking the books, maybe helping themselves to some of the ready?"

"It's too early to tell," she said. "But Deacon Tom, who is an accountant had just been tasked by Father Vince and the Parish Council with doing an audit and trying to figure it out and report back."

"Interesting," Joe said. "One of the first rules of detecting, after 'cherchez la femme,' that is, is 'follow the money.'"

They pulled into the Church parking lot and walked through the front door of the Rectory. They asked for Father Vince, and were shown into a small waiting room, furnished with old-fashioned furniture, somewhat time-worn. On the walls were the obligatory framed pictures of the Pope, the Bishop, and the previous pastors of the parish. The opposite wall contained a framed Knights of Columbus Charter and an Apostolic Blessing from Pope Pius XII in 1950. Father Vince entered the room, looking nervous and worried. Meg waited for Joe to take the lead, since he had seniority and she was only an Acting Detective, detailed to help him. Nevertheless, he greeted her first.

"Hi Meg," he said. "I didn't expect to see you, and out of uniform." She explained her status on the case to him, and introduced Joe.

"I'm sorry to disturb you at a time like this," Joe said, "but I'm sure you understand that we have to interview everybody who knew the victim, and especially those who worked closely with him. Since you probably worked more closely with him than anybody, we're starting with you, but we will also have to interview your entire staff in the rectory, and the school."

Father Vince nodded. "I'm still trying to process it. It's just so unbelievable," he said. "He was such a nice guy, well-liked by everybody."

"I'm sure he was in general, but clearly somebody must have disliked him, or feared him, enough to kill him. It's our job to find that person, and we need your help," Joe responded.

"I'll do everything I can, but I just don't know. He didn't have any enemies that I know of. Of course, there are always arguments around a parish, and sometimes they're heated, but they don't rise to the level of homicidal rage."

"I understand, but sometimes somebody can touch a raw nerve, get too close to a guilty secret, for example. We have to look for things like that, and to do it, we have to know everything, no matter how small it seems. Tell us about these 'arguments.'

"Well..." Father Vince hesitated, clearly reluctant to get into it. "We will be discreet, Father," Meg said. "I already know quite a bit about it, but I'm a detective, not a witness. We need to hear it from you, as well as from other involved witnesses." Father Vince looked at Meg as he spoke. He seemed to be more comfortable addressing her, even though she already knew most of what he was going to say.

"It's like this. The parish school has a cash flow problem, to the tune of about $40,000. We were just informed of this recently. It has become necessary to transfer $40,000 from the parish account to the school account. They are actually separate entities--separate corporations, in fact, so this caused some consternation, you might even say some hard feelings, on the parish council. We had a rather stormy meeting the other night." He turned to Joe. "Meg was there," he explained. "She is on the parish council."

Joe nodded. "Explain to me why there were hard feelings, and on whose part," he said.

Father Vince contemplated his hands, and gathered his thoughts. "Well, it pains me to say it, but the parish is sort of divided into those who support the school, and those who don't. It's kind of, but not completely, an age thing. I guess," he said. "People who have children in the school naturally assign a high priority to the school. They believe that handing on the faith to the children is the most important thing that we do, and that the school should get priority in regard to the parish's assets," he explained.

"On the other hand, we have a declining population, our congregation is ageing, there are fewer young families with children. There is not as much support for the school as there used to be. Some of the senior citizens and empty-nesters resent the amount of money spent on the school. Not all of them, but a substantial number. So, there is always a controversy over the amount of subsidy from the parish to the school."

"But is this serious enough to kill somebody over?" Joe asked.

"No, of course not," Father Vince replied. "But things did get very heated. The thing is, this was unexpected. We had already given the school their subsidy for the year. Suddenly, they discover that they have a cash-flow shortage of $40,000, and they weren't going to be able to make payroll. Some members of the council were very suspicious. There were some nasty accusations."

"So there is a possibility that somebody has their hand in the till?" Joe speculated.

"I really don't think so," Father Vince said. " There is a logical explanation, having to do with slow tuition collection. Still, some of the council members were suspicious. We delegated Deacon Tom, who is, er, was, an accountant, to do an audit of the school's books."

"This is something we're going to have to look into more," Joe said. "But it really doesn't sound like motive for a murder."

"No, I'm sure it isn't," Meg said. "It doesn't make sense."

"Was there anyone else that Deacon Tom had a problem with?" Joe asked.

Father Vince looked at Meg and then back at Joe. "Well, he and Bruce Poole used to butt heads over spending on the music ministry. Bruce is the music minister," he explained. "He's very focused on himself and his concerns. He has no concept of a budget. It was Tom's job to say 'no' to him, and they used to clash, but it was business, it wasn't personal, and again it wasn't a motive for murder."

"Had Deacon Tom started his work on the audit?" Joe asked.

"Yes," Father Vince answered, "but he couldn't have gotten very far into it yet. I'm sure he hadn't come to any conclusions, or he would have told me."

"OK, Joe said. "Can you think of any other questions, Meg?" he asked.

"Not at the moment," she responded, "but I'm sure things will come up after our other interviews, Father. We will check back with you then."

Father Vince stood up and shook hands with both officers. "Do you have any idea when the body will be released," he asked.

"The autopsy is scheduled for one o'clock. I should think the funeral home will have it by tomorrow," Joe said.

"I'll do anything I can to help." he said. "I have to go and see Sheila later this morning and discuss the funeral. I'm not looking forward to that."

CHAPTER 7

BACK IN THE CAR, JOE AND MEG LOOKED at each other with an awkward moment of silence. Neither knew exactly how to break the ice. Finally Joe decided to take a shot at it.

"It's great to be working with you, Meg," he said. "It's going to be a bit dicey for us both, though. I mean, we'll have to keep our personal relationship and working relationship separate, if that's possible. I'm kind of surprised that the Inspector put us together."

"I imagine that he doesn't know we're dating," Meg said. "There's no reason he would. I haven't discussed it with anybody at work."

"Neither have I," Joe said. "I wonder if we should tell him."

Meg though for a minute. "I don't think it's relevant," she said. "He may eventually hear about it through the grapevine, but after all, lots of cops date each other. Let's wait and see if he brings it up."

"You're probably right," Joe said. After a pause, he continued, "You do still want to date me, don't you Meg?"

Meg's immediate thought was: 'This guy seems like a keeper. Most cops are drunken philanderers. He seems different. I'm not letting him get away this easily.'

"Of course I do, Joe," she said. "I don't see any reason why we shouldn't, that is if you still want to," she said.

He exhaled a sigh of relief and looked at her fondly. "Of course I do," he said.

"Well now that we've got that out of the way, what's next on the agenda?"

" I suppose we should interview the Principal and the Assistant Principal," Meg answered.

"Do you know them?" Joe asked.

"Yes," she answered. "They're both ex-officio members of the parish council, for one thing, but I've known Sister Moira for years. I think she's been here since the First Vatican Council. But Rick Peters is fairly new, a couple of years, I think. He seems to be doing a good job and getting along well with people."

Joe started up the car and drove to the school, entering the parking lot from the Downing Street entrance. They exited the car and entered the school and climbed the stairs to the second floor where the

Principal's Office was at the top of the landing. As the secretary ushered them into Sister Moira's office, she rose from her desk to greet them.

"Meg, I'm surprised to see you here," Sister Moira said. Joe and Meg looked at each other and grinned, sheepishly.

'We're going to go through this with every interview,' Meg thought to herself.

"Meg has been detailed to work with the detectives on this case because she knows all of the players, and knows the lay of the land, so to speak," Joe explained.

"Of course, I see that," Sister Moira said.

"Sister, this is very early in the investigation, and we're trying to get as much information as we can about Deacon Tom, his relationships with the people and employees of the parish, and what exactly he was doing and working on in the days before his death," Meg said.

Sister Moira grimaced. "Was this really a murder, then?" she asked.

"I'm afraid so," Meg said. "His head was bashed in with a blunt instrument. He was hit from behind," she said. "That isn't what he died from though. He died from carbon monoxide poisoning. But he was knocked unconscious first, and then the gas feed was deliberately disconnected from the boiler, filling the room with gas."

"Oh my God, it's so horrible! I just can't wrap my mind around it. I can't imagine who would do such a thing," the sister exclaimed.

"Yes, well, everybody says the same thing, but the fact is that somebody did do it. It's our job to find out who and bring them to justice," Joe said.

"Yes, and what makes it worse," Meg said, is that the perp is probably somebody we all know. Random tramps don't go around wandering into school boiler rooms and disconnecting gas feeds and hitting clergymen over the head. This was a premeditated act, and there has to be a motive. Our first step is to discover what it was."

"O dear, it's so distressing," Sister Moira said. "Well, what can I do to help?"

"First of all, what was Deacon Tom working on in the days before his death? What was going on in his life, as far as you know?" Meg asked.

"Well, as you know, we have a financial crisis of sorts in the school. I guess it's called, in accounting-speak, a 'cash-flow shortfall.' To make a long story short, we're about $40,000 short of cash, and we wouldn't have been able to make payroll without the cash transfer from the parish. Although I accept Rick's explanation of the reason for it, there are those on the parish council who didn't, who insinuated that there is something amiss, some 'cooking the books' as one council member referred to it. As a result, as you know Meg, Deacon Tom was commissioned to do an audit of the school finances and write a report for the council of the exact cause of the shortfall."

"So that's what he was working on. How far did he get?" Joe asked.

"Yes, that's what he was working on, and I don't know how far he'd got, but I would think he was just getting started. I can't imagine he was very far into the details yet. Rick was working with him. He'll know more about that than I do."

"Yes, we'll interview him next," Meg said. "Did you have much contact with Deacon Tom?"

"Yes, a fair amount," Sister Moira said. "He was sort of the general manager of the parish. Finance, building maintenance, equipment purchasing, managing the parish staff, these were all among his duties, so he was around quite a bit. He had his eye on everything."

"Was there anything in particular that you know of that he was looking into just before he died?" Joe asked.

'Not other than the audit, but he was a very busy man, I can tell you that. He had his fingers in everything that went on. He worked so hard to serve our Lord."

Her voice started to falter, and her eyes started to tear-up. "Oh dear, I just can't believe it. It's so hard to process. You're quite sure it was somebody he knew?" she asked.

"We have an open mind. We'll go where the facts take us," Joe said. "But right now, everything points that way. There's no way to explain this as an accident, nor is it likely that a someone just wandered in off the street and committed all these acts for no reason."

Sister Moira shuddered. "Well, all I can do is pray for Deacon Tom's soul, and pray that you find out quickly who did this. This is a tremendous strain on al the parents, students and teachers. People are talking about nothing else. The teachers tell me they can't get any teaching done. They're spending all their time con-soling the students. Everybody knew Tom, and he was very well loved."

"I know, Sister. We're working very hard on it, and you can be sure that we'll get to the bottom of it," Meg said.

"Well, that's all the questions we have now," Joe said, "but if you think of anything else, be sure to contact us right away. Anything at all. You never know what little piece of information could be useful."

Joe and Meg stood and took their leave. As they came down the stairs, Joe said: "Let's take a look at the boiler room. We may see something that triggers a question or an association."

When they reached the ground floor, they walked down the corridor, past the cafeteria, and opened the door to the boiler room. The CSI people were finished with their work, and the crime-scene tape had been removed. As soon as they entered the boiler room they were on an iron platform. They descended six iron steps to the floor level. The boiler was straight ahead. On the concrete floor, they could see the chalk outline of Deacon Tom's body. It was only about eight paces from the bottom of the stairs to the boiler. They had to speak in a loud voice to hear each other over the humming of the machinery.

"Well, this explains why he didn't hear his attacker creeping up on him," Joe said. "This machinery would drown out a lot of sound."

"But what was he doing down here in the first place? That's what puzzles me," Meg said.

Joe looked around. "I think he must have had some reason to think there was a malfunction with the boiler," he speculated. "He comes down here, he kneels down to check the boiler out, and the perp creeps up behind him and hits him over the head with something, maybe a wrench. Deacon Tom falls unconscious, then the perp disconnects the gas feed and leaves him to die from asphyxiation."

Meg shuddered. "But why?" she asked. "I not only can't imagine who would do it, I can't imagine what the motive would be."

"In this case, I think when we know the motive, we'll know the culprit," Joe said.

CHAPTER 8

BY THE TIME THEY FINISHED EXAMINING
the boiler room scene, it was lunch time. They decided
to go to Mudd McGuire's for lunch, a pub a few blocks
down the street from the school. It was a hangout for
cops after hours, but now it was full of neighborhood
people, and employees from Mercy Hospital across the
street, on their lunch hour. Joe and Meg walked through
the bar to the back room and took a quiet table in the
corner. They had been dating for a couple of months,
but most of their friends and work colleagues didn't
know it. They were both still a little bit nervous about it.
There were loads of romances between cops, but many
of them didn't stand the test of time--and the stress
of the job. The waitress approached, and without even
consulting a menu, they decided to split a large order
of chicken wings and a pitcher of diet pepsi. Chicken
wings were the specialty at Mudd's. After hours it

would have been a pitcher of beer, probably Labatt's Blue, but there was no drinking on duty.

Meg broke the ice. "I have a lot of mixed emotions about this assignment, Joe. It's a big chance for me. I'm fourth out on the list for detective, so I'll be reachable any time now, and I feel like the Inspector is giving me a trial. I appreciate that."

"I sense a 'but' coming," Joe said.

"Yes." Meg responded. "The 'but' is that I was very fond of Deacon Tom, and this matter is very personal to me. Also, many of the people whom we have to question are friends of mine. For that matter, it's very likely that the perp is going to turn out to be somebody I know. It's very awkward, and a bit scary." These thoughts had been running through Meg's head ever since the inspector gave her the assignment. It was a huge relief to share them with Joe. She felt so comfortable and natural talking to him about it, both because he was a good detective and because he was a good man.

"I know what you mean, Meg," he said. "But it won't be the last time that will happen to you. We work in a big city, but the South District is in some ways like a little village in Ireland. These people have been marrying their first cousins for generations. They're all related to each other."

Meg burst out laughing. "You have a point, but it's not quite that bad," she said.

"Oh no?" Joe retorted, "this neighborhood is like Lisdoonvarna. Some days, I feel like I'm acting in a scene from 'The Quiet Man.'"

"Which character are you, John Wayne or Victor McLachlan?" Meg teased.

"Well, I'm not your brother, so I must be John Wayne, right?" he retorted.

"And I'm Maureen O'Hara?"

"Well, you don't have red hair, but..."

They laughed, and then they were both quiet for a moment.

Meg took a sip of her Diet Pepsi. "We really didn't get much useful this morning, did we?" Meg asked.

"Not really," Joe said, "but we'll have to follow up on this financial audit angle. I figure this afternoon we'll keep working our way through the parish staff. We've got no 'persons of interest' outside the parish at the moment. We might as well start with the music director. He seems to have quarreled with the vic. Do you know him?" he asked.

"Yes," Meg said. "He's kind of a twit. Full of himself, and full of drama. But I have difficulty picturing him doing this. He doesn't have the nerve or the strength."

"Well," Joe replied, "somebody did it, even though they all look unlikely at the moment. We've got to interview them all and get their statements."

Their food came, and they were silent while they worked their way through the plate of wings. There is no genteel way to eat chicken wings. You just pick them up in your fingers and start gnawing the meat off the bone, often getting the sauce on your face while you're doing it. Not a good choice for guys with beards.

"Tell me what you know about this organist dude," Joe said. Meg wiped her mouth with a paper napkin, and took a sip of her drink while she reflected.

"Well, his name is Bruce Poole. He's been at the parish for about three years. Before that he worked at several other parishes in the city. He's a graduate of the Eastman School of Music, which he will tell you within minutes of meeting him. He's very full of himself, kind of a prima donna. Very fussy about his music. He's more than an organist. He will be very quick to point out to you that he's the 'Director of Music,' in charge of all the music efforts of the parish. He directs the choir, the folk group, and he teaches music to the middle school kids."

"Somebody mentioned that he had a quarrel with the vic. Do you know anything about that?" Joe asked.

"A little bit," Meg answered. "It came up for some discussion on the Parish
   Council."

She thought for a moment before continuing. "What I remember hearing is that he wanted to hire some kind of a special music group to play at the Easter Vigil Mass. Their fee was a bit steep, so he had to get approval, and Deacon Tom, who was in charge of overseeing budget and finance, was having none of it. We have plenty of volunteer music talent in the parish, and Tom told him to use that. Bruce was not pleased, and was grousing to everybody who would listen."

Joe was pensive for a minute. "Kind of petty," he said. "Doesn't sound like much of a motive for murder. Does this guy have a short fuse?" he asked.

Meg thought. "He can be very irritable when he doesn't get his way," she said. "But I don't see him as violent. He's more verbal than anything. I should have said he's kind of a cream puff."

"Well, we'd better have a go at him and see where it takes us," Joe said. They settled their bill and got into the police car for the short drive back to the parish complex. They found Bruce Poole in his office, between the church and the rectory.

"Hello Meg, I'm surprised to see you here," he said.

Meg had to tell the story all over again about being detailed to the Detective Division to help with this case, etc. 'I'm going to get sick of explaining this before we're through,' she thought to herself. She introduced Joe and explained the purpose of their visit.

"I'll cooperate with you in any way I can," Bruce said. "But Deacon Tom and I weren't very close, and I don't know how I can be of any help."

"We're interviewing everybody who had any dealings with him, especially in the last days before his death," she said. "I understand you had a bit of a dust-up with him the day of the parish council meeting."

Bruce grimaced. "I wouldn't call it a 'dust-up'" he said. "I put in a request to hire a special music group for the Easter Vigil Mass. After all, it's the most important liturgy of the year. It's very important that it be very correct and liturgically well done."

"And what did he say," Joe asked.

"His position was simply that we didn't have the money. Apparently Rick Peters had just given him some bad financial news about the school, and he was in a foul mood. He more or less said that I should make do with the resources we have."

"Well, wasn't that reasonable?" Joe asked, more to see what kind of reaction he could provoke than to elicit information.

"The parish folk group is bloody awful. They're still playing a repertoire of maudlin folk songs from the Seventies. Hold hands and sing Kumbaya stuff. Not at all suitable for the Easter Vigil, one of the most important liturgical services of the year," he said in a huff.

"Well, how did you leave things with him," Joe asked.

"He rather abruptly said the answer was, 'No,' and that was final, and I said I don't accept it and I would talk to Father Vince about it."

"And did you?" Joe asked.

"Not yet. There hasn't been an opportunity, and now, well, obviously it wouldn't be the time."

"No, I don't think it would," Meg said. "Best to drop it. The Easter Vigil is going to be very subdued this year."

"Did you have any other dealings with him recently, other than the request to hire a special music group?" Meg asked.

"No, I really didn't," Bruce said. "We weren't BFF's. We didn't have much in common. He wasn't very interested in music or liturgy, except when it concerned the budget. That was his fixation. He was a bean-counter, after all," Bruce said slyly.

"You mean an accountant?" Meg asked.

Bruce made a face. "Yes, that's exactly what I mean," Bruce responded.

"How did he get along with the rest of the staff of the parish," Joe asked.

Bruce looked pensive. "He seemed to get along reasonably well. He was a bit stressed out about the financial responsibilities, and could be grumpy about it, but I don't know of any feuds with anybody."

"Is there anything else you can think of? Anything that might help us?" Joe asked.

Bruce thought for a moment and then said, "Not really. I don't know of any real enemies that he had. He could be a little bit annoying, but that's all. I can't think of anybody wanting to kill him," Bruce said. "I can only surmise that it was something random. Maybe some homeless person got into the school, and Deacon Tom caught him, there was a struggle and he was hit."

"That seems very unlikely," Joe said, "but we'll keep it in mind. "Keep thinking about it, and if you think of anything, anything at all no matter how insignificant it seems to you, give us a call."

CHAPTER 9

BACK IN THE POLICE CAR, THEY DIS-
cussed their next move. The afternoon was already
growing late. "Do we squeeze in another interview?"
Meg asked.

"I don't think so," Jose said. "I think we should go
back to the Station, type up all of these interviews, and
conference with the Inspector. By that time, he will
probably have some information for us on the autopsy,
CSI reports, etc. which may point us in one direction
or another,"

"Sounds like a plan," Meg said. "By the time we
finish that it will be quitting time."

Returning to the station house, they each fortified
themselves with a cup of strong station house coffee,
and sat down at computers to begin typing up the notes
of their interviews. After typing quietly for a little over
an hour, they each printed out their notes and began to
compare them.

Meg frowned and shook her head. "It doesn't seem like much to go on so far," she said.

"No, it isn't," Joe said. "But the strongest line of inquiry so far seems to be this matter of the cash short-fall. It could be just slow tuition collection, as they think, but on the other hand, if somebody helped himself to forty large and Deacon Tom found out or was close to finding out who did it, that would be a strong motive for murder," he observed.

"True, but since Tom was going to do an audit and now he's dead, how do we find out if there was some sort of theft or embezzlement?" Meg asked.

Joe sat in silent thought for a moment. "We'll have to speak to the Inspector. We should report the day's business to him anyway. He'll have to decide how to get our arms around this business of the school funds. The Police Department may have to hire its own auditor."

"Can we do that?" Meg asked.

"I don't know," Joe said. "That's what the Inspector is getting paid the big bucks for. I suspect he'll have to consult the D.A."

Joe picked up the phone and dialed the Inspector's number. When the Inspector answered, he said:

"Inspector, this is Joe Curry. Ryan and I have been interviewing witnesses all day at St. Brendan's on that homicide. We've got our notes written up, and we'd like to talk to you about where to go from here." After a brief exchange he hung up. "The Inspector wants to see us right away," he said.

They gathered their notes, and left the squad room and headed for the stairwell. Inspector Flanagan's office was on the second floor of the station house. In its former life, it had been a switching office for New York Telephone Company. After switching offices became superfluous, the building was put up for sale, and the city bought it and turned it into Police Station for the South District. It was old and the room configuration was Byzantine, but it worked, more or less.

As they entered Inspector Flanagan's office, he motioned them to take seats. They sat in the two chairs facing his desk. "Now, how are you getting on?" he asked.

They briefed him on the day's interviews. "Well, you've talked to the three people in the parish who probably had the most contact with him, and they were cooperative. How useful their information is remains to be seen," the Inspector said. "So where are you at this point?"

"Well," Joe said, "looking at the traditional big three: motive, means, and opportunity, lots of people probably had opportunity, but we have to know the time of death before we can ask people where they were at that time, so we have to await the autopsy report.

"In terms of means, we need to know the cause of death. It appears that the proximate cause was carbon monoxide poisoning. It appears that he was knocked unconscious by a blow to the head with a blunt instrument first. It could have been any of the tools laying around the boiler room: a wrench, a hammer, a lead pipe. So we also need the autopsy report for that, as well as the report from the CSI people. Was any blood, hair, etc found on any of the tools in the boiler room?"

"No," the Inspector answered.

The Inspector asked, "Given what you know now, do you see any fruitful lines of inquiry, any path forward, so to speak?"

"Well, that brings us to motive," Joe responded. "Deacon Tom seems to have been pretty well liked by everyone. There were some arguments, but they don't seem serious enough to be a motive for murder. But two themes recur, such as they are.

"The first seems rather minor, but the deceased got into a dispute with the music director over money to hire a music group, and it got rather heated. They parted brass rags, both determined to push the point further.'

"Doesn't sound like much," the Inspector said. "Music people are always a pain in the ass."

"We agree, sir. The second one seems more substantial, and to get to the bottom of it, we may need to take custody of the school's books and do our own audit somehow. That's what we wanted to talk to you about it. I'll let Ryan explain that piece to you. She understands it better than I do," Joe said. He thought it was time Meg picked up the ball and had an opportunity to show the Inspector her stuff.

"OK, Meg, what's the story?" the Inspector asked.

"Well, sir, it seems that there is a shortfall of about $40,000 in the school's accounts. The school had to come to the parish council last week and ask for a $40,000 loan to make payroll. Needless to say, there was a big uproar. The Assistant Principal, Rick Peters, had an explanation, having mostly to do with slow tuition collection, which sounded plausible. But about half the parish council believed it, and half didn't. There were accusations, demands for an audit, tempers got hot. The result was that Deacon Tom, who is, or was, an accountant, was directed to do an audit of the school's books. He had just started on the audit when he was killed. I don't think he'd got very far, but I don't know."

The Inspector thought. "Hmm. If somebody did dip into the till to the tune of forty thou, obviously it could be a powerful motive. We need to dig into that further," he said.

"Our thoughts exactly, Inspector," Meg said. "to do that, we need two things: we need the schools accounting ledger, checkbook, etc., and we need the services of a forensic accountant. As far as the books go, do we just ask for them, do we seek a subpoena, or do we seek a search warrant? And how do we get the services of a forensic accountant?"

The inspector's eyebrows rose. "Well, we don't have anywhere enough evidence to get a judge to sign a search warrant, not to mention the fact that the Mayor and the Commissioner would have my scalp if I even suggested it."

"We could just ask them for the books and they'd probably give them to us, but how would we know if we got everything?" Meg said.

"Exactly. So I think the way to go is to ask the D.A. to issue a subpoena," the Inspector said. "Also, the D.A.'s office has forensic accountants who they retain for jobs like this, guys who are used to testifying in court and giving expert opinions. I'll speak to the chief of the Homicide Bureau at the D.A.'s Office and ask for a subpoena *duces tecum*, and also ask them to find a forensic accountant to review the books for us."

Meg looked puzzled. "What is a subpoena *duces tecum*?" she said.

"*Duces tecum* is Latin for 'bring it with you,'" the Inspector said. "We're not asking anybody to come and testify, we're just asking them to give us the books and records."

"How long will that take?" Joe asked.

"Not very long at all, the Inspector answered. The D.A. can issue it in the name of whatever Grand Jury happens to be sitting right now. We should have them in a day or two. I can't imagine that the Church will resist the subpoena. They'd have to go to court with a Motion to Quash. That wouldn't put the Church in a very good light. I'm sure they'll just give them to us. After all, they want to know the answer to the same question that we do."

Exactly," Joe said. "So tomorrow, we'll just keep going down the list of witnesses to interview at the parish, right sir?"

"Right. Keep me posted at the end of every day, like you did today." the Inspector confirmed.

"Yes, sir," Joe and Meg said in unison.

CHAPTER 10

WHEN THEY ARRIVED BACK TO THE Detective Office it was end of shift time. Meg and Joe packed up their notes and their laptops and got ready to leave for the day. Meg felt all wound up, both because she was interested and involved in the case, and because it was exciting working with Joe, but a little bit nerve wracking at the same time. She didn't know how it would work out, working every day on something as intense as a murder investigation with somebody she was dating and starting to have romantic feelings for.

"Do you have any plans for dinner?" Joe asked.

"No, I'm all at sixes and sevens," she said.

"How about if I pick you up at seven and we'll get some dinner at The Dove?" Joe asked.

"Sounds good. That will give me time to shower and change and unwind a little bit," she said.

Meg entered her apartment, picked the mail up from the floor where it had fallen through the mail slot, and checked the answering machine. There was a message from Kathy Meegan. Rosemary had recovered fairly quickly in the hospital. She was kept overnight for observation, but was now home and feeling normal again. Meg said a swift prayer of thanksgiving. She removed her work clothes and took a quick shower. Then she took her hair down form the regulation police "bun," and brushed it out into her normal "do." She then went through her closet, trying to decide what to wear to dinner. "Something feminine," she though, "not pants." She wanted Joe to regard her as a colleague, but not as "one of the boys." She held up a few dresses and rejected them, and then finally decided on a dark green dress, cut just above the knees. Sleeveless, but not low-cut. She wanted to convey just the right message: attractive, but modest and professional. She accentuated it with a gold scarf, tied around the neck in the current French style. A pair of black patent leather pumps, a touch of lipstick, not too much, and she was ready.

She sat down to wait for Joe, and picked up the latest book she was reading. She was addicted to British mystery novels. This one was called *A Mourning Wedding* by Carola Dunn. She only had to wait about 15 minutes when the doorbell rang. She opened the door and Joe was standing there, looking very handsome in a blue button-down dress shirt, a tweed sport coat and black dress pants. "Just right," she thought to herself. "not only good-looking and fun to be with, but he has class and good taste besides."

He gave her a light kiss on the cheek. She closed the door and they walked to his car, a Ford Escape, where he opened the door for her and held it while she entered, throwing her into a state of some mental confusion. 'How do I handle this dating somebody I work with as a partner,' she asked herself. 'At work, I have to be independent and professional. We can't be seen to be acting in any way romantic on the job,' she mused. 'But after work, he's clearly courting me, and I'm enjoying it.'

They arrived at The Dove Restaurant, and were shown to a table in the corner, partly shielded by an aspidistra. "I wonder if he arranged this," Meg thought.

A waiter came and took their order. They each had a glass of Malbec, followed by a field green salad and shrimp scampi.

As they were making their way through the salad, Joe said, "Well, let's take stock of where we are. We've interviewed three witnesses, and nothing much came of it except the clear sense that we have to follow up on this business of the cash shortfall. The Inspector is taking care of getting a subpoena for the parish books, and getting a forensic accountant to go over them and give us a report, so we can leave that for the time being."

"Right," said Meg.

"So tomorrow we continue to work our way down the witness list. Who do you think we should interview, and in what order?"

Meg thought for a moment, taking a sip of Malbec to aid the cogitation process. "Well," she said, "We should probably do Rick Peters, the Assistant Principal next. He's at the middle of this whole business about the money."

"Right," Joe agreed. "What then?"

"We have to interview Grace O'Neill and Becky Nowak. They are two parents who were in the school yesterday morning, and set the whole thing in motion by noticing the smell of gas and giving the alarm. And we should interview Bob Glinski, the school custodian. He's all over the school all the time, and takes care of the boiler, among many other duties. He would know better than anybody if anybody has been hanging around the school who shouldn't be, and might be able to give some insight into how this happened, when and where it did," she said.

She thought some more and added, "For that matter, he might be able to shed some light on what Deacon Tom was doing in the boiler room in the first place. Although he certainly had the right to go there, the question is, 'Why would he?'"

"Very good point," Joe said. "In fact, next to the money issue, it may be the key to the whole mystery. What was Deacon Tom doing in the boiler room at that time of the morning?"

They finished their salads and sat in silence for a few minutes.

"Well, that's a pretty good work program for tomorrow," Joe said.

"Yes, it should take us a good part of the day, if not the whole day," Meg responded.

"Also, we should receive the autopsy report tomorrow," Joe said. "We'll have to review that and see where it leads us, if anywhere. Also, the body will be released and there will be a wake and funeral to occupy people."

"Yes," Meg mused. "Should we attend the wake and funeral?"

"Absolutely," Joe said. "In a murder investigation, you always attend the wake and funeral. It's a good opportunity to observe the people in the deceased's life, and see how they react and interact. Sometimes you pick up a helpful lead."

"The funeral will be packed," Meg said. "He was very well-known and well-liked, and I'm sure many of his brother deacons and priests will attend."

"Yes, well, we'll sit in the back and just observe the faces and the body language and see if anything helpful presents itself. Sometimes it does."

The main course came, and Meg and Joe devoted their attention to the food for the next few minutes. Shrimp scampi was one of the specialties at The Dove, and it definitely lived up to its reputation.

When they finished eating and moved on to the coffee, Joe broke the ice. "Tell me about your family. Your Dad was on the job wasn't he?"

"Yes, for twenty-five years," she said. "All of it on patrol in A District, where we're working right now."

"What was he like?" Joe asked.

"He was a wonderful Dad," she said. "He really loved his wife and children, his faith, his city and his parish. He taught us about duty and responsibility, loyalty and perseverance. He was not a philanderer, like many cops."

Meg began to tear up. Joe looked at her quizzically. "I sense a 'but' coming," he said softly.

She nodded. "The 'but' is that the job took a toll on him. He saw so many horrible things. Dead bodies. Bodies maimed in all kinds of horrible ways. Suicides. People who hung themselves, or blew their brains out. You know how it is."

Joe nodded, but said nothing.

"He never lost his gung-ho spirit. He was often the first on a call, the first into the house, and so often the first to see a body of a homicide victim, a suicide victim, or an old lady or man who had been dead for a week, with the flesh rotting and the stench unbearable. He used to tell me that he always dreaded 'check on the welfare' calls."

"Yes, we all do," Joe observed. "You never know what you're going to find. The call usually comes in because somebody hasn't been seen or heard from for days, isn't answering the phone, etc. Too often you have to break in, and you find a dead body."

She nodded. "Yes," she said. "He retired after twenty-five years, but the job stress had taken a physical and mental toll on him. He suffered from what we now call PTSD, but it was undiagnosed and untreated, because he never went to the doctor and never opened up to anybody about it, except sometimes my mother."

"He never talked about it in the presence of us kids, but he used to talk to my mother about it after we were in bed. Sometimes I overheard. He used to have night-mares. He would wake up shouting as if he were at the scene of a homicide or a suicide or an accident. I think he thought the suicides were the worst. He just couldn't wrap his head around why anybody would take his own life. Toward the end he couldn't sleep. He used to be up a good part of the night pacing, restless.

"He died from a heart attack, fairly young, at age sixty. I feel that it was brought on by job-related stress."

Joe took her hand and squeezed it. "You're prob-ably right," he said. "The statistics show that cops have a high incidence of heart attacks, and they often don't live very long after they retire."

They both sat in silent reflection for a few minutes. Then Joe said, "If you don't mind me asking, why did you join the force, having seen what you saw and knowing what you know about what it's like?"

She reflected for a moment. Tilting her head, she replied, "I think partly out of respect for him, partly a desire to follow in his footsteps, and partly out of a desire to serve, to help people."

"It's funny," she said, "I've worked with some old-timers who worked with my Dad. They've said things to me like, 'you're a chip off the old block,' or 'the apple doesn't fall far from the tree.' That gives me a good feeling, a proud feeling. I can't think of anything nicer than to be told I remind someone of my Dad."

There wasn't much to be said after that. The sat holding hands in silence for a good, many minutes. Then Joe paid the check, escorted Meg to the car, and drove her home. When they said goodnight on her doorstep, he kissed her on the mouth--until they both needed to come up for air.

CHAPTER 11

RIGHT AFTER THE NEXT MORNING'S
Detectives Meeting in the Station, Meg and Joe began
to interview the witnesses on the work program they
drew up for the day. They started with Rick Peters,
the Assistant Principal of the school. Father Vince had
given them an office in the Rectory to use for their interviews. Shortly after 9:00 AM they were both seated
behind a small conference table as Peters entered. They
waived him to a seat. They had agreed that Joe would
begin the interview to keep it on an official basis, since
Meg knew him socially.

"Mr. Peters, I'm Detective Curran, and this is Acting
Detective Ryan. As I believe you know, we are investigating the murder of Deacon Tom Flynn, and we need
to ask you some questions," he began. Peters looked at
Meg with confusion on his face. He knew her as a uniformed P.O., and was unaware that she had been pro-
moted to Acting Detective. His eyes moved from one

to the other in a nervous manner, but he leaned back in the chair and tried to act relaxed.

"Murder? Are you sure it wasn't an accident?" he asked.

"Yes, we're sure, Joe said. "The autopsy has confirmed it. He was hit over the head with a blunt instrument, and knocked unconscious, and then the gas feed to the boiler was deliberately disconnected, spewing gas into the boiler room. He actually died from carbon monoxide poisoning."

"Well, I'll cooperate in any way I can, but I don't know how I can help," he said.

"We're interested in the financial problem in the school. We understand Deacon Tom was working on an investigation of that commissioned by the Parish Council at the time of his death. I wonder if you could tell us, from the beginning, what that was all about."

Peters looked around nervously. "Hey, wait a minute, his death couldn't have had anything to do with that," he said.

Meg tried to speak in a soothing voice. "I'm sure it didn't, Rick, but we have to build the whole picture, so to speak. We have to look at everything, reconstruct the last days of his life, and then start eliminating things that aren't relevant. Surely you understand that."

He exhaled a sigh of resignation. "I guess so," he said uneasily. "As I've told everybody over and over again, it's simply a cash-flow shortfall. Times are tight. People aren't paying their tuition on time.

"We only have a few families who are what we call 'full-payers,' who pay the full sticker price. Most families apply for and receive some sort of financial aid. This was not fully budgeted before I got here. A certain amount was budgeted for financial aid, but the amount of financial aid given exceeded the amount budgeted. This had been going on for several years," he explained.

"Besides that, only a very few families pay fully in advance at the beginning of the year. The vast majority of families pay monthly or quarterly. If they choose to pay monthly, they're supposed to enroll in automatic deduction from their checking account, but some families refuse to do it. They say they'll pay monthly by check, and then some of them don't, or they're habitually behind a month or two or three. All of these things have been going on for years too. Cumulatively and gradually, these factors have started to add up to a big problem. Our tuition collection doesn't coincide with our regular monthly obligations, especially payroll."

"I see," said Joe. "When did you discover this?"

"I discovered it virtually the day I started on the job," he said. "I did mention it to Sister Moira any number of times, but she has no head for finance. Numbers befuddle her, and she just said 'God will provide, my dear.'"

"So, did you tell anybody else about this problem," Joe asked.

"Well, Sister Moira is my boss. It was her job to take it up the chain of command. It wouldn't be my place to go around her directly to the pastor, would it?"

"I suppose not," Joe responded.

"I did bring the general problem of slow tuition collection up at a number of Parish Council meetings, but for the most part, nobody had anything constructive to offer. A few council members just made comments like, 'Keep after them Rick.'"

"I had always been able to deal with it by 'robbing Peter to pay Paul,' so to speak. Not paying bills on time, deferring expenditures until the next month or the month after, calling up parents and pushing them to get their tuition in. It was a slowly developing train wreck, but finally the day came when we were going to be unable to make a payroll. It's not that I wasn't warning them, but nobody was listening," he pleaded.

Joe looked at Meg and she nodded slightly. "OK," he said. "We have retained a forensic accountant to take over the audit that Deacon Tom had started, and we might have more questions for you as that progresses or when we get the results."

"On another matter, how well did you know Deacon Tom?"

"Well, I had to deal with him on financial matters, of course, so he was around a lot, but it was strictly business. I don't live in the parish, so I didn't know him socially at all, and I didn't see him much outside of work, except at Parish Council meeting and a few other events for the school. We weren't buds, and I don't have much to do with the school after hours."

"Did you ever have any quarrels with him," Joe asked.

"No, not really. We had a few words over this recent budget matter. He didn't seem to fancy my explanation of the cause of it. I was upset that he questioned me, but not unduly. I knew that the facts would bear out my explanation in the end. School finance is not complicated really. On the revenue side tuition is seventy five percent of the total. Fundraising and donations are the other twenty five percent. On the expense side, payroll is seventy five percent of the total. After that you have insurance, utilities and supplies. Everything else is pennies. It's not complicated at all."

Joe decided to change the subject.

"How long have you been here at St. Brendan's," he asked.

"Three years," Peters replied.

"Where did you work before that?"

"I taught Math at St. Malachy's School, on the East Side."

"Why did you leave?" Joe asked.

"Better opportunity. I had earned my Administrator's License by going to grad school at night and summers. This assistant Principal's job came up and was posted on the Diocesan website. A promotion, more responsibility, higher salary. I applied, interviewed with Sister Moira and Father Vince, and got the job."

"Who was your boss at St. Malachy's?"

"Sister Claire Duquin."

"She would give you a good recommendation?"

Peters looked startled and somewhat nonplussed. "Of course," he said. But he didn't seem well-pleased at the question.

"We'll have to check with St. Malachy's. Routine, of course. It's standard procedure to check out all the key witnesses. That will be all. We know where to reach you if we need any more information from you as the investigation progresses."

Peters got up with an irritated look on his face, turned and left the room.

Joe looked at Meg after he left. "What do you think?" he said. "You know him."

"Not very well," Meg said. "As he stated, he doesn't live in the parish, and doesn't come around after hours, except for Parish Council meetings once a month."

"I can verify the part of his story about warning the Parish Council of slow tuition collections. I do recall him bringing it up in a general way. He never warned us of an imminent crisis, but he did bring the problem up in a general way several times."

"And what happened?" Joe asked.

"Nothing. Nobody wants to talk about financial problems. Especially at Parish Council meetings, and especially problems that don't have an easy solution. They'd rather talk about the length of the homilies, or complain about the music at the 9:00 Mass, or the length of the 4:30 Mass," she said.

"We don't get any of that at my parish," Joe said.

Meg looked at him in surprise. She assumed he was Catholic because he was Irish. There were other little signs, such as he knew how to address clergy, etc. But they had never discussed religion. It was on her agenda before they got any more involved, so she was glad that he gave her an opening.

"Oh? What is your parish," she asked.

"I go to the Latin Mass at St. Anthony's, downtown," he said. "The Mass is an hour and a half, the hymns are all in Latin, the homily is a minimum of twenty minutes, and nobody complains. Then we have a buffet breakfast afterwards in the Hall. It pretty much takes all morning."

This guy is full of surprises, she thought.

"That's very interesting," she said. "You'll have to tell me more about that."

He looked at her with a twinkle in his eye. "Over dinner and a bottle of wine. It's a long story," he said.

"Deal" she said. "You bring the wine and I'll cook the dinner."

CHAPTER 12

MEG AND JOE HAD ARRANGED FOR TWO of the school Moms, Becky Nowak and Grace O'Neill, to meet them in their temporary rectory office after lunch. Becky and Grace were at school that fateful morning and had sounded the alarm when they smelled gas. Prior to the meeting Meg and Joe compared their notes for a bit.

"Becky and Grace probably have more promise, in that they may have been actual eyewitnesses to something helpful. They were in the school at the time that the whole thing started."

"Good point," Joe said. "If they had actually seen a smoking gun, I assume they would have said something by now. But they may have seen some little thing that they didn't realize was important."

"Right. Although they're both very sharp. Grace is a lawyer. She is trained to pay attention to detail."

"Well, let's start with her," Joe said.

Meg left to fetch Grace O'Neill, and returned with her a few minutes later. She was dressed attractively but professionally, in a blue plaid skirt and a red pullover, stockings and black pumps. Her long, shiny, black hair was pulled back and held by a clip behind her neck. She sat down casually and crossed her legs. Meg introduced Joe and explained what they were about.

"I understand. I'll do whatever I can to help you," she said.

"I understand that you and Mrs. Nowak were in the school when all of this started to go down. I'd like you to take us through that morning. Tell us what you did, what you saw, what you observed, just like you're telling a story."

"Okay," she said calmly. "Becky and I were in the school. We were set up with a table outside the cafeteria. We were preparing to sell gift cards to raise money for sports uniforms. We are there every Friday from 9:00 to Noon. Parishioners drift in and out to buy the cards. "

"Had anyone come in yet," Joe asked.

"No, not yet, We had just set up. It was a little after nine. One of the cafeteria ladies came out and asked us if we smelled gas. We had just noticed it ourselves. We said yes, we thought it was coming from the stove in the cafeteria. She said she had checked that and it wasn't. We all noticed that it seemed to be stronger near the door to the boiler room, which was across the hall from us.

"Just around that moment, Sister Moira, the principal, came down the stairs from her office and asked us if we smelled gas. We said 'yes, and it seemed to be coming from the boiler room.' She said she was going to go into the boiler room and check. I said 'that's not a good idea. Just call the Fire Department. That's their job.' She did, and they told her to pull the fire alarm and get the kids out. So that's what we did. We evacuated, and took the children across the street to the Church."

"When you were in the school, did you see any strangers around, anybody at all that didn't belong there?"

"No," she said. "There was nobody there but employees. Nobody had showed up to buy cards yet."

"Was there anybody in the halls who shouldn't have been?" Meg asked.

"No, no one. The children and teachers had just come over from Mass and entered their classrooms. The cafeteria ladies were there, of course, in the cafeteria. Bob Glinski, the handyman/maintenance man was walking around, carrying mops and tools, doing what he does, but nobody else."

"I see. And you saw nobody go in or come out of the boiler room?" Joe asked.

"No. No one," Grace responded. "The door was closed, and we saw no one go near it."

Joe thought for a minute. "You say you were there every week selling these gift cards. Did you ever see anyone go into or out of the boiler room?"

"Oh yes," Grace answered easily. "Bob is in and out of their all the time. It isn't just a boiler room. All the cleaning and maintenance tools and supplies are kept there. In addition to that, some of the older boys were apparently assigned to help him with light cleaning. Sometimes you would see one or two of them. But no one on the day in question."

"Fair enough," Joe said. Changing the subject, he asked: "Tell me about this maintenance man. How well do you know him?"

"Not well," Grace answered. "I see him around here a lot, and I always speak to him but just a few pleasantries. He's a veteran. He was in the military for quite a while. More than one enlistment, I know that. He was wounded in Afghanistan. I believe he got some sort of medical or disability pension. I've heard that he goes to the VA Hospital for some sort of treatment. I believe Father Vince knows somebody in his family. He was looking for a job, he's very mechanically inclined, so Father Vince hired him."

"Okay, we'll be talking to him too. Right now we're just collecting statements from everybody who could possibly have seen or known anything. There is a limited number of people who could have done this."

"Couldn't it have been an accident?" Grace asked.

"I'm afraid not," Joe said. "Deacon Tom was bashed in the back of the head with a blunt instrument, and the gas feed was deliberately tampered with. There's no question of accident.

"It's just hard to believe that it was someone that we know," Grace said with a shudder. "Could it have been an intruder, a burglar perhaps?"

"Possible but very unlikely," Joe answered. "It's hard to believe that some tramp wandered in off the street, into a school boiler room, bashed a clergyman in the head and tampered with the boiler, releasing carbon monoxide into a school with 320 students."

"Besides, in an investigation, you start with the most likely scenarios first, and eliminate possibilities one at a time, until you either have an answer, or hit a brick wall."

"I know," she said. "It's very distressing to think there was a murder where your children go to school."

"Yes. I urge you to keep thinking about this, and if anything comes to mind that you might have forgotten, get in touch with Meg."

Grace took her leave, and her place was taken by Becky Nowak, whose testimony was almost identical, and produced nothing new.

Meg and Joe finished up, discussed what they had and had not learned, entered their notes into their laptops, and packed up their things.

"What's on the agenda next?" Meg asked.

"Well, we go and report the day's activity to the Inspector, and then you and I will consult, like Sherlock Holmes and Dr. Watson. Or Hercule Poirot and Captain Hastings."

"Ah, yes, you promised to explain to me how you came to be a devotee of the Latin Mass," Meg said.

"And I think you promised to cook dinner," Joe replied.

"So I did, and so I will," Meg agreed.

"My place or yours?" Jo asked.

"Mine. I cook best on my own stove."

"Fine. I'll bring the wine. Do you prefer white or red?"

"Red," Meg answered.

"Good. I'll bring a nice Malbec. See You at seven?"

"You've got it," Meg said.

CHAPTER 13

MEG HAD SHOWERED, CHANGED INTO A plaid skirt and a green blouse, fed her cat, Gilbert, and begun to plan the dinner. She had decided to make linguine carbonara, one of her specialties. She fell in love with the dish when she was on pilgrimage to Rome several years earlier. It is the local specialty of the Romans. She made a point of learning how to properly prepare it the Roman way and loved to serve it to guests.

She took the ingredients out of the refrigerator, and lined them up on the counter so they would be ready. She poured some heavy cream in a small cream pitcher, broke two raw eggs in a small bowl and beat them, put a kettle of water on the stove, on a burner turned very low to start to slowly come to a boil for the linguine, and put some pancetta in a skillet to saute when the time came. She also got out a big wooden salad bowl, filled it with romaine lettuce, croutons and anchovies to create a Caesar salad. All that was needed was to add the dressing at the last minute.

While her hands were busy, she took the opportunity to reflect. She realized that she was at a turning point in her life, in more ways than one. First of all, she knew that she had been given a tremendous opportunity by being made Acting Detective and allowed to work on a homicide case. She realized that if she and Joe were able to solve the case, it would be an enormous boost to her career. Why had the Inspector given her this big chance, anyway? He said it was because she knew the players, but she didn't sense that was the complete answer.

And then there was Joe. She was developing deep feelings for him, and she believed she saw signs that he was reciprocating those feelings. But Joe was an enigma. She didn't really know very much about him. She was surprised to hear him say he went to the Latin Mass. In her mind, people who went to Latin Mass were sort of uber-Catholic. And you had to go out of your way. It was only offered in two parishes in the entire city. She hadn't even known if he was Catholic until that comment. She had sort of assumed he was because he was Irish. It sort of went with the genes, but she hadn't been sure.

She was very serious about her faith, but she realized that in some ways she had always taken it for granted. It sort of came with the package if you grew up in an Irish family, she thought. She had sort of drifted away when she was in college, and then a few years ago she had experienced a conversion, or more accurately a "reversion," at a retreat for young adults, and later a girlfriend had convinced Meg to accompany her on a pilgrimage to Rome. Meg had at first regarded it as a sort of tourist vacation, but had been deeply moved by the atmosphere of majesty and holiness that permeates the "Eternal City." She felt a spiritual reawakening that had remained with her ever since, and had motivated her involvement in St. Brendan's parish life.

Her thoughts worked their way back to Joe. She felt that they needed to have a serious talk about how they felt and where their relationship was going, but at the same time she felt she had to tread lightly. She didn't want to seem too forward. Guys were like young colts; they spooked very easily. But, neither did she want to waste time. Her biological clock was ticking. She needed to know how Joe felt about marriage, and about children. In her view, the purpose of dating was to find a husband. She wasn't going to keep dating somebody for years who had no intention of getting married.

On the other hand, she wouldn't marry somebody who wasn't open to children. And she wanted to know how he felt about careers. She wanted children, but she also wanted to keep working. What would it be like being married to another cop, especially when the children started coming? She knew a lot of cops were married to other cops. Some of them worked out well, but some did not. There was also a lot of infidelity and promiscuity in the Police Department. So much to discuss, and the sooner, the better.

The doorbell rang. She glanced at the clock. Just gone 7:00. Punctuality is a virtue, she thought. But she still didn't have her thoughts sorted out. Oh well, she muttered a quick prayer to the Holy Spirit for discernment, and resolved to wing it.

She opened the door, to find Joe standing on the porch with a bunch of red roses in one hand and a bottle of red wine in the other. He kissed her on the cheek, as she took the roses from him and led him into the kitchen. She got a vase from the cupboard, and went to the sink to fill it with water, arranged the roses and placed them on the dining room table, which was already set for two. "They're lovely, Joe," she said, as he took her into his arms and kissed her, this time on the mouth, with an intensity that left no doubt about his feelings.

"Come in the kitchen and talk to me while I make dinner," she said. They stepped into the small kitchen, and Joe perched on a stool while she began to put the meal together. She began to saute the pancetta in the skillet. She brought the kettle to a boil, and put the linguine in it to cook-*al dente*. After nine minutes, she poured the linguine into a strainer to drain, and then poured it into a big bowl. She added the pancetta, beat the eggs, and poured them into the hot pasta, while simultaneously pouring in the heavy cream with the other hand. She then mixed it all together with two large forks.

She dressed the Caesar salad, and handed it to Joe. "If you will put that on the dining room table, I'll bring the Carbonara. It has to be served hot. The heat from the hot pasta is what cooks the eggs and cream into a sort of sauce. This is the way they do it in Rome, where Carbonara is a signature dish. That's where I learned it."

Joe uncorked and poured the wine, an Argentine Malbec, and they sat down at the table. They glanced at each other sheepishly for a moment. "Shall we say Grace?" Jos asked. Meg breathed a sigh. She was just wondering whether to suggest the same thing. This was a good sign.

"This is absolutely delicious," Joe said after the first few forks full. "You said you learned how to make this in Rome? What were you doing there?" he asked.

"I went on a pilgrimage with a girlfriend a few years ago, and I absolutely loved it. In Italy, every city has its signature dish, and Carbonara is Rome's. It's usually made tableside by the waiter. A chafing dish of hot pasta is brought to the table, then the pancetta, eggs and cream are slowly folded into the hot pasta, which cooks it instantly."

"Tell me about Rome," he said. "I've never been there."

"It's fabulous," she said dreamily. "So much history, so much atmosphere. There's a church every few blocks, all extremely old. Hundreds of years old, some, like Santa Maria in Testevere, or San Clemente, go back to the first centuries A.D. And many of them have bodies of saints entombed in a crypt or under the main altar, and in a number of cases, such as St. Cecelia, the saint's body is incorrupt."

"That's impressive," Joe said. "I've never been there. I'd love to go someday. I've always thought it would be a great place for a honeymoon."

'Mmm. If this is meant to be an opening, it's big enough to drive a truck through,' Meg thought. 'Better not let it go.'

"A perfect place. If I got married, I'd love to go to Rome with my husband on our honeymoon" she said. "We could get a Papal Blessing We could have Mass at the Tomb of St. Peter, tour the Sistine Chapel and the Vatican Museum. There's so much to see," she said.

She gazed at Joe. He was looking at her like he wanted to say something, but didn't know how. 'Guys need so much help, she thought. They're so brave about some things, but so intimidated around women. It's too bad we don't have professional Matchmakers in this country, like they used to have in Ireland.' He seemed to suddenly make a decision.

"Meg, what do you think about the dating game?" he asked.

She drew in a breath. Her heart was pounding. Either this was going to be great, or it was going to be a deal-breaker.

"Well, I'm afraid I'm terribly old fashioned. I don't believe in serial dating," she said. "I believe the purpose of dating is to find a spouse."

It was Joe's turn to exhale. "That's exactly what I believe," he said. The door was opened, and the serious discussion began.

It was a long evening, and they made the most of it.. By the time they finished talking, about everything from their childhood, to their families, to their careers, to their dreams about the future, their desire for children, their views about big weddings vs. small, the raising and education of children, and much more, the candles on the table had burned down a good three inches.

When Joe finally got ready to leave, they both felt like their life had entered a new phase. The good-night kiss was a long one.

CHAPTER 14

THE NEXT MORNING, AFTER THE START-of-shift briefing in the detective's Squad Room, Joe and Meg sat down to plan their day. They had made arrangements to meet with the balance of the Parish Council members at staggered times in the small Rectory office they had commandeered.

"First we've got Marty O'Connor, president of the Parish Council, then we've got Lester Nestorious, leader of the opposition, and then we've got Joe Browne, Jim Curran and Judge Sadowski, all on the same side of the aisle as Lester.

"Opposition? Opposition to what," Joe asked with a puzzled look.

"To whatever we're doing at the moment," Meg answered. "It doesn't matter whether it is in the parish, in the diocese, or in the Church as a whole, whatever we're doing, they're opposed to it. It's like a mini-parliament, and they're the backbenchers. But, the silver-lining is, that we may get more out of them than other witnesses, because they have their ears fine-tuned for gossip."

There was a tap on the door and the secretary stuck her head in. "Marty O'Connor is here to see you," she said and stepped aside for Marty to enter the room.

Joe and Meg stood up to greet him. "Hello, Meg," he said.

"Hello, Marty, this is Joe Curry," he is assigned to investigate this case and I am detailed to work with him," she explained.

"Well, I will help you in any way I can. This is a terrible thing. Nothing like this has ever happened here before," Marty said.

Joe waived him to a seat and they all sat down. "What we're interested in from you is mainly background," Joe explained. "Fill us in on what you know about Deacon Tom, everything you can think of. How long he's been here, where he came from, who he hung out with, anybody he might have quarreled with, that sort of thing."

"Well, he's been here, I don't know, maybe four or five years," Marty said. "He's an accountant who took early retirement from his firm due to some heart issues, and decided to devote his life to full-time diaconal ministry. He did sacramental things like baptisms and weddings, assisted at Mass, and preached homilies on occasion. He ran the RCIA program, but he mostly functioned as *de facto* parish business manager. He saw to all of the practicalities that Father Vince didn't have time for or wasn't good at."

"Who were his friends?" Joe asked.

"Well, he was friendly with nearly everybody, but he didn't have any best buds that he hung out with, or anything like that. You know, it doesn't do for members of the clergy to have favorites or get involved in cliques. They have to try to just be on good terms with everybody, but not be seen to 'hang out' with one group or another," Mary answered.

"Fair enough, who didn't he get along with" Joe asked.

Marty though for a minute. "I wouldn't exactly say there was anybody he didn't get along with. But you have to understand that his job was to manage the parish budget. That meant that he had to say 'no' to people. To tell them that they couldn't have money for their latest project, they couldn't have the parish hall the same night the Boy Scouts had it, that sort of thing. People got a little testy about that from time to time."

"And do you know who was 'testy' with him recently?" Joe asked.

Marty grimaced. "Well, Bruce Poole, the organist *cum* music director, to begin with," he said. "He had a grandiose idea of hiring some outside music group to provide music for the Easter Vigil Mass at a cost of about nine hundred bucks, I think, and Tom was having none of it. He's in charge of the budget, and he put down his foot and refused to allow it. Bruce was livid."

"How did you learn this?" Joe asked.

"First of all," Marty said, "Bruce was running around complaining about it non-stop to everybody who would listen. But Deacon Tom and Father Vince both gave me a heads-up as Parish Council President, so I got it from all sides."

"And what was your take on it?" Joe probed.

"I supported Tom completely. First of all, we put him in charge of the budget, so we have to back him up. We can't have people doing end-arounds to the Pastor or the Parish Council. Secondly, he was objectively correct. The expenditure is not in the budget, and given the financial condition we're in, we can't be spending nine hundred dollars on an outside music group. He wanted to hire a folk group. I wouldn't be for it if they offered to pay us. Ridiculous," he snorted.

"I see. How upset was Bruce?" Joe asked.

"It's hard to say. He's always in a snit about something. That's the type of personality he has. But nothing ever comes of it. It would be nice if he'd throw a hissy fit and quit, but he won't. He just whines and complains. Nothing ever comes of it. I don't think you're going to find a motive there. It's not important enough."

"Probably not, but at the beginning everyone is a suspect. We collect all the information we can on them, and then we rule them out one at a time, just like a doctor doing a differential diagnosis. Anybody else?"

"Well, of course there was Rick Peters and the flap over the financial problem at the school. A cash-flow shortfall, he calls it. But that's a fancy name for deficit, isn't? If the budget was balanced at the beginning of the year, and it was, then where did the money go?"

"That sounds like a good question. Where does he say it went?" Joe asked.

"Basically, he says it never came in. Slow tuition collection, he says. That's why he calls it a 'cash-flow shortfall.' His position is that it will come in, it's just a 'timing imbalance,' he says."

"And what's your position?"

"I don't have one," Marty said. "Rick may be right. But we have to look into it, don't we? And that was the job Tom was working on when he died."

"Fair enough," Joe said. "Well the D.A.'s Office has now hired a CPA firm to go over the books and we'll have to await their report before we go too far down that rabbit hole. Anything else we should know?"

"No, there really isn't," Marty said. "I don't know of any juicy scandals, going on. It completely baffles me. I can't think of any reason why anybody would attack Tom. Nor for that matter can I think of any reason why he would go into the school boiler room. He has keys to everything, and he's sort of second in command, so he can go anywhere he wants, but he's not at all mechanically inclined. I can't think why he'd go in there."

"Yes, that seems to be puzzling everyone. Well, we've sort of set up shop in this office. If you hear of anything at all that might be useful, let us know," Joe said.

Marty shook hands with Joe, gave a smile and a nod to Meg, and made his exit.

After he left Joe gave Meg a quizzical look. "That was about what I expected," Meg said, "and it's a pretty true and objective account of the situation around here.

Marty is a good chairman, he steers a middle course and stays away from any factionalism."

"Yes, so it seems. Well, who's next?" he asked.

"Lester Nestorious," Meg said. "He's the leader of that 'loyal opposition' I mentioned this morning."

"The controversy of school funding is rearing its head again right now because of the cash-flow issue.

"And then there's always the liturgy," she continued. "It never takes much to get a good fight started about that."

"That's one more reason why I love the Latin Mass. Long history. No controversy," Joe replied.

"That's true," Meg responded. "I sometimes wonder why Lester and his fellow 'opposition members' haven't jumped ship for one of the Latin Mass churches. He and his cronies form a loud but not very large group who sometimes refer to themselves as the 'Trads.' They want to go back to the pre-Vatican II Latin Mass, with all of its trappings and flourishes. It's also more than that. The opposition manifests conflicts in many ways. For example, there are arguments over whether hymns should be sung in Latin or English, whether incense should be used, etcetera. There seems to be an infinite number of things to fight over in liturgical matters," she said.

"In all fairness, I must admit that there have been many unauthorized liturgical abuses since the Council, too. One hears stories about hootenanny Masses, Cabbage Patch vestments, priests coming off the altar and strolling up and down the aisles playing the guitar and singing folk songs, girls in tutus doing liturgical dance during Mass, all of these things have happened."

Joe stared at her with his mouth open. "Good Lord," he said. "I feel like Rip Van Winkle. I must have been asleep. I had no idea any of this has been going on."

"Well, I suppose that's a good thing," Meg laughed. "Anyway, that's what we're about to encounter, I'm sure."

There was a tap at the door, it opened and a thin man with short-cropped grey hair and glasses dangling off the end of his nose, entered. He was dressed in a white shirt and blue and gold striped tie, a grey cardigan and neatly pressed dress slacks. He registered surprise at seeing Meg. "What are you doing here, Meg," he demanded.

"I'm detailed to work on this case. This is Detective Joe Curry. We're working together on it. Please sit down, Lester," she said.

He looked displeased, but took a seat.

"We're investigating the murder of Deacon Tom, and we just want to ask you a few questions," Meg said.

"Why me? I don't know anything about it," he said defensively.

"There's nothing to be alarmed about. We're just collecting background information at this point. We're interviewing everybody on the parish council, and all of the parish and school employees too. We just want to ask you a few questions."

"All right, I'm sure I'll help you if I can," he said cautiously.

"First of all, did Deacon Tom have any enemies that you know of?" Joe asked.

"No, I wouldn't say so," Lester answered. "He was sort of the de facto parish business manager. He was in charge of overseeing the budget, purchasing, mainte-nance and use of the parish facilities. His job involved saying 'no' to people, about spending money, com-peting demands on the facilities, and so on. The people he had to say 'no' to would sometimes get annoyed and grumble, but that was all."

"He was kind of a friendly, likeable guy. He had heart trouble and high blood pressure, and stress could get to him sometimes, but I don't know of anybody who had it in for him."

"Had he quarreled with anybody recently?" Joe asked.

Lester's brow wrinkled, and he paused a moment before answering.

"Well, you have to understand that there are always quarrels around here," he said. "You might think a church should be one big happy family, but it's not. There are quarrels over budget, fund-raising, use of the buildings, music, liturgy, even the decorations. But they don't really amount to anything serious. Not anything that somebody would kill over."

"Any examples of who he quarreled with lately?" Joe asked.

A thin smile crossed Lester's lips. "Well, first of all, there was that poof of a music director. He wanted to spend nine hundred dollars to hire a rock band for the Easter Vigil Mass. Deacon Tom vetoed that, and rightly so. The idea was ridiculous."

"Then there was the whole kerfuffle over the school funds. There seems to be forty thousand dollars missing. There was a big to-do about it at the last parish council meeting, and Deacon Tom and Rick Peters, the Vice Principal, got a little heated about it. The result was that Deacon Tom was tasked with auditing the school books and getting to the bottom of it. I would definitely start there if you're looking for a motive."

"What do you mean 'forty thousand dollars missing?' Are you saying there was a theft?" Joe asked.

"No, I'm not saying that. They're calling it a 'cash-flow shortfall.' And it may be. The way it was left is that Deacon Tom was directed to audit the school books and give us a report at the next meeting. Now he's dead, with his head bashed in. It seems to me that's a place to start looking. If there is forty thousand dollars missing, that's a sizeable motive," he said.

"You can be assured we are looking into it," Joe said. "Is there anything else you can think of that would be helpful?" Joe asked.

"Not at the moment," he answered.

"All right then, Lester, if you think of anything that would be helpful, we'll be here until the investigation is completed."

Lester rose and made his exit.

"What next?" Joe asked.

"We've got three more witnesses on standby, but it's nearly one o'clock. "Why don't we get some lunch and tell the secretary to have them come at two?" Meg suggested.

"Good idea. I'm starved. Let's go to the Blackthorn."

"You read my mind," Meg said.

CHAPTER 15

TEN MINUTES LATER, MEG AND JOE WERE sitting at a corner table in the Blackthorn Pub. Joe had a cup of coffee in front of him, and Meg had an iced tea. The waitress came to take their order. Joe ordered a Reuben, and Meg ordered a chef's salad.

"Well, where are we?" Meg asked.

Joe thought for a minute. "Well," he said, "we really didn't learn anything new, but it was all useful to me as background information, because I'm not as familiar with the cast of characters and the lay of the land as you are. I do have a better picture of the situation than I had before."

"Yes, I guess I agree," Meg said thoughtfully. "It's hard to believe that the school budget is a motive for murder, but as weak as it is, it's the best line on a motive that we have so far."

"I agree," Joe said, "but on the other hand, it's out of our hands at the moment. The D.A.'s Office has an accounting firm auditing the school books, and until we get that report, we don't know whether we've got a smoking gun or a tempest in a teapot. So we have to just put that aside for the moment and follow other leads."

"Well, the only other thing we've got at the moment, silly as it seems, is the dispute with Bruce Poole over the money for the music group. It certainly doesn't seem important enough to be a motive for murder," she said.

"No, it doesn't," Joe said. "But we have to follow it up. I think, more than the dispute itself, we need to look into Poole's background. He seems to have a strange personality, to say the least. Check with his prior employers. See if he had any history of violence, or erratic behavior."

"I agree," Meg said. "Even though the motive itself seems trivial, if Bruce is looney tunes, perhaps anything could trigger him. It doesn't have to be logical."

"True enough," Jose. said. "So we certainly need to look deeper into friend Bruce's background. Nevertheless, I think we're missing something. There has to be more possibilities than these two."

The waitress brought their food, and they put the case aside and concentrated on filling the void in their stomachs for a few minutes.

As he was finishing his Reuben, Joe looked at Meg and said: "Tell me more about your Dad."

Her face brightened immediately.

"He was a wonderful Dad," she said. "Very strong, very moral. He loved his family and he loved the job, even though it gave him a lot of stress at times."

"He was in the Vietnam War, in the Marines. He was wounded over there. I don't know much about it. He would never talk about it. I know he got the Purple Heart, and the Bronze Star. I still have all of his medals at home. They're mounted on a plaque on my wall."

"That was a tough war," Joe said. "Those guys didn't get the respect they deserved when they came home."

"No," she said wistfully, "and in later years he suffered PTSD from it, as well as from things he saw on the Police Department. He was getting treated by the VA, and he had to take medication for it. He would have nightmares, sometimes he would have flashbacks and think he was still in Vietnam, and wake up in the middle of the night shouting and trembling. My mother would have to calm him down."

"That must have been awful for you," Joe said.

"Well, it was scary the first few times I saw it. But once he got diagnosed and got treatment, it didn't happen that often, and my mother was very good at dealing with it.

"He loved police work, even though it caused him stress at times. He was a good street cop. Cool under fire, but very good at defusing a tense situation. He never lost his temper."

"How long was he on the job?" Joe asked.

"Twenty-five years. He got a regular service retirement. But he died way too early, from a heart attack. I can't help but feel that his Vietnam service as well as his police career contributed to it. As I mentioned before, he was only 60 when he died. Way too young."

"I'm sorry," Joe said. "I know he is proud of you now, Meg, and that he is watching over you."

"Well, if the good Lord lets him, I hope he gives me a clue to help solve this case!" Meg smiled.

CHAPTER 16

BACK IN THEIR TEMPORARY OFFICE IN the rectory, Meg and Joe reviewed their morning notes and prepared for their afternoon interviews. On the agenda were Judge Sadowski, Jim Curran and Joe Browne.

Glancing over the list, Joe said: "Do you think we can get through these in an afternoon?"

"Maybe not, but we'll see," Meg said. "a lot of it is going to be repetitive." It turned out that the three parish council members, Judge Sadowski, Joe Browne and Jim Curran, testimony pretty much mirrored that of Lester Nestorious. They had no specific new information to offer, but they all pushed the theories that Lester had introduced: that the only two people with a motive were either Rick Peters, if he were 'cooking the books', or Bruce Poole, based on the nonspecific notion that he had a miserable personality and somewhat irreverent tastes in liturgical music. They were unable to explain how that would be a motive for murder, except the vague notion that everyone finds him annoying.

At then end of the day, Meg and Joe were exhausted, but felt no further along in terms of the investigation, except that they had crossed a number of interviews off their list. But those interviews seemed to produce no information that got them any closer to a solution. As they packed up, Meg said, "Well tonight is the wake for Deacon Tom, and tomorrow is the funeral. Perhaps they will yield some helpful surprises."

"Absolutely," Joe said. "You never know what you might learn at wakes and funerals. Especially when it's an Irish wake. It's a goldmine of gossip, which some-times provides useful information."

Joe looked at his watch. "It's 5:15. The wake starts at 7:00. Should we get a bite to eat?"

Meg smiled. "I thought you'd never ask. Lead the way," she said.

CHAPTER 17

A HALF HOUR LATER, MEG AND JOE WERE seated at a corner table in Mollie's Pub, grabbing a quick dinner before heading to the wake.

"What do you think of today?" Meg asked.

Joe took a sip of his Guinness. "Well, it was a good day's work. We learned more about the cast of characters and what they're like. But we didn't get any closer to finding a motive.

"No, that's true," Meg said. "It seems that everything hinges on that accountants' report. If they come up with proof that there's actual cash missing, it could be a strong motive, and it would pretty much point to Rick Peters. But if not, we've got nothing. Apart from the fact that Deacon Tom ruffled some feathers in the course of doing his job, he seemed to be beloved by everyone."

"True," Joe said. "Bruce Poole didn't like him, but that isn't enough of a motive for murder. Bruce seems to be a prickly fellow who doesn't like anybody who prevents him from getting his way."

"A stranger seems to be ruled out as well," Meg said. "Becky and Grace were sitting right there in the middle of the hall, in 'Times Square' you might say. Nobody could have entered the building or gone into the boiler room without going by them."

"True," Joe said.

The food came. They had each ordered Shepherd's Pie, a house specialty, washed down with Guinness, a pint for Joe, a half for Meg. They ate in silence for the next fifteen minutes.

Meg, was thinking of her years on the force and was grateful that she had come from good stock. She had a difficult time of it in the Police Academy with the physical requirements, and there were a few times when she secretly questioned whether she would aspect, and almost didn't make it. But with stubborn determination and a lot of support from a lot of people, including a girlfriend who was a doctor and a cousin who was a physical trainer, she made it. On graduation day, as she was being congratulated by Captain Mahoney, the Academy Director, she confided her fears to him.

"I never had any doubt that you would make it," he assured it. "Oh?" she said with surprise, why was that?"

"Because you are your father's daughter," he answered. "You're a chip off the old block." Meg considered that one of the nicest compliments she had ever received, but she also knew that it was really a compliment of her father.

So, since she was indeed her father's daughter, she decided to take the bull by the horns and continue their discussion from the other night at her home about marriage and family.

"Joe," she said, "what do you think about kids?"

Joe kiddingly looked around like somebody had set off a stun grenade in the bar.

"What do you mean, what do I think about kids?" he smiled.

"Well, you know, we are Irish. Be fruitful and multiply, and all that stuff."

"To be honest with you," more seriously now, he continued, "When I was a kid I always dreamed of having a big family."

Her eyes lit up. "So did I," she said. "I always thought seven would be a good number,"

"How did you come up with seven?" he asked.

"Oh I don't know. Seven is said to be the biblical perfect number, you know. I just came to me, and it felt right."

"I see," he grinned. "And are you prepared to bear seven children?"

"Oh yes, God willing. And my husband."

Joe laughed out loud. "Yes, he'd have to be willing too. And he'd have to work a lot of overtime. Do you have somebody in mind for that job?" Joe mischievously asked.

"Ah now, that would be telling," she laughed. "I do hear it said that there's a lot of overtime in Homicide, though," she said.

Joe smiled. "Well, it's time to head to the wake. We'd better put on our serious faces," he said. "Speaking of faces, watch the faces and the body language, as well as eavesdrop on every conversation you can. And go to the ladies room often. You have the advantage over me there. Men spend about 60 seconds in the Men's Room and don't talk about anything. Women go to the loo in two's and three's and four's, and talk about everything. Listen to it all."

CHAPTER 18

THE WAKE, LIKE 99% OF ALL CATHOLIC wakes, was from 7:00 to 9:00 PM. But as Joe and Meg rolled up to McSorley's Funeral Home at 6:45, the parking lot was already almost full, there was a traffic jam, and two uniforms were attempting to direct traffic. One of them spotted Meg and Joe, and waved them into a reserved parking spot near the door. As they entered the funeral home, there were a lot of people milling about, and there was a long line waiting to view the body and pay their respects. Deacon Tom's wife and two adult children were standing next to the casket, accepting condolences from mourners while heroically trying to listen to their small-talk. Meg, suddenly and uncharacteristically thought of something funny, and had all she could do to keep a straight face. Joe noticed immediately, and said: "What's up?"

She leaned over and whispered to him: "If one of those little old Irish ladies from the parish comes in and walks up to the casket and says, 'Sure and doesn't he look just like himself,' I'm going to bust a gut." Joe looked shocked. "They wouldn't do that, would they?" he asked. "Are you kidding? You can bet on it," Meg said.

Joe just grinned and shook his head.

"Look," he said, "let's split up. Let's each engage as many people as possible in conversation, and eavesdrop on as many conversations as possible. You'd better drink a lot of water so you can a lot of trips to the Ladies' Room. Take your time putting on your make-up or whatever you girls do in there, and listen to the gossip. You never know what little tidbit may be useful."

Meg smiled. "OK," she said. "I'm going to go up and pay my respects at the casket and console the family first. After all, I did know him pretty well."

As Meg started walking over toward the casket, Tom's wife Sheila spotted her and came toward her with her hands outstretched.

"Thanks so much for coming, Meg," she said. "Oh you're welcome," Meg said. 'What does one say at a time like this,' she thought. They both walked up to the casket. Deacon Tom was laid out in his diaconal vestments, alb, stole and dalmatic. He looked very peaceful. The undertaker had done a good job. The wound, which was on the back of his head, was of course not visible. Sheila introduced Meg to the couple's two adult children, Brenda and Matt, and Meg expressed her condolences. Meg knelt down on the prie-dieu that was in front of the casket, and said the traditional Our Father, Hail Mary and Glory Be, followed by the formulaic prayer for the dead that the nuns had taught her: "Eternal rest grant him O Lord, and may your perpetual light shine upon him." Then she made the Sign of the Cross and rose to her feet. Another Catholic ritual. It's what one does.

Sheila looked at her. "Is there..." she began. Meg shook her head. "Not yet," she said. "But we're working on it night and day. It's like building a wall. One brick at a time. We're interviewing a lot of witnesses, trying to build a mosaic. We will solve it, Sheila, I promise you that."

Sheila nodded. "I know you will," she said.

"I won't keep you," Meg said. "A lot of people are waiting to talk to you. I'll keep you posted as we go along," she said.

Meg spotted Rick Peters in the corner, and drifted over toward him. He was standing alone, looking very uncomfortable. She approached him.

"Hi Rick, how are you doing?"

"Awful, if you want the truth," he said. "I feel miserable. I feel like everybody is looking at me."

"Oh it's your imagination, Rick," she said. "Why do you think that?"

"Come on, Meg. You know I was one of the last people to speak to him, and we had a rather public spat over the school's cash-flow problem. Tom had picked up the school's financial records from me and was doing a so-called audit. Next think anybody knows, he's dead on the boiler room floor. Everybody is speculating on a motive, and I am the favorite target of most of them."

"Well I wouldn't worry about it, Rick," she said. "You know that we have a CPA firm doing the audit now, and we'll know soon if it was just a cash flow problem, and then there will be no reason for anybody to look in your direction."

"I hope so, but the problem is, there doesn't seem to be any other direction to look in. Deacon Tom got along with everybody. As far as anybody is aware, he didn't have any enemies. I'm a nervous wreck over it. I can't concentrate on anything."

Meg almost felt sorry for him. But she had to admit that he was the prime suspect. What could she say?

"Stiff upper lip, Rick," she said. "We're putting a lot of resources into this case, and we'll solve it soon."

"I wish I were confident of that," he said.

She disengaged herself from Rick, and looked around the room. The room was long, with the casket at one end of it. There were two doors, one intended to be the entrance and one, the exit, so that people were expected to enter through the door nearest the casket, pay their respects and say a prayer at the casket, and then exit through the other door. However, there were so many people that the whole room looked like a huge Rugby scrum. Meg looked around and spotted Bruce Poole standing by himself near the exit door. She dove into the crowd and made her way over to where he was standing by himself, looking very uncomfortable.

"Hello Bruce," she said amiably. "How are you?"

He gave her a sideways look. "Are you here to pay your respects or to detect?" Bruce asked. "I see you working the crowd."

"It's what one does at Irish wakes, Bruce. Besides," she said with a wry smile, "I'm a woman. I can multitask."

"I suppose so," he grunted. "So how is the investigation going?"

"It's early days. We're just interviewing everybody who knew him, taking statements, trying to put together a mosaic. You know, 'When did you see him last?' 'Where were you between the hours of…' all that sort of thing. Trying to put together a picture of what he was like, whether he had any enemies, what were his relationships like, etcetera," Meg replied.

"Are you getting anywhere?" he asked.

"It's too early to tell, but a picture is gradually emerging. What do you think, Bruce?"

"Me? How should I know? Why ask me?" Bruce responded with some agitation.

"Well I'm sure you've been thinking about it. You must have some ideas. Who do you think could have done it?"

He looked at her as if taking her measure for the first time. Then he said:

"Let's not beat around the bush, Meg. I know I have to be a prime suspect. It's well known that he and I quarreled. I wanted to bring in professional musicians for the Easter Vigil, and he didn't want to spend the money. My job is to provide liturgical music that is…relevant, and inspiring and inclusive. His job is to watch the pennies. We were bound to clash. But it wasn't something that anybody would kill over, for God's sake. That's ridiculous."

"Well then why bring it up, Bruce?" Meg asked.

"Because I know people are gossiping about me. I know that certain members of the Parish Council have it in for me because of my...tastes. But it's ridiculous to think that I would kill anybody. I abhor violence. And the issue between us was nothing more than an annoyance. Organists and Musical Directors are in high demand. I can get another job any time I want."

"Well then I wouldn't worry about it Bruce," she said. "Put it out of your mind. People are always going to gossip about something. Don't pay any attention to it."

"Yes, easier said than done," he grumbled.

"Excuse me, I have to use the Ladies' Room," she said. 'I think I'll make one of my trips, and check that box off,' she thought to herself. After she used the toilet, there were several other women standing at the mirror fixing their makeup, so Meg joined them and fiddled with her compact and lipstick. Wrapped up in their own conversation, they weren't paying any attention to her. Meg recognized Mrs. Connors, one of the sixth grade teachers, and Mrs. DelMonte, the school secretary. She listened.

"What was Deacon Tom doing in the boiler room, that's what I want to know," Mrs. Connors said. "I never knew him to go down there before."

"What I think is," Mrs. DelMonte said, "he saw somebody going down there who shouldn't have been, and he went in to investigate, saw the boiler had been tampered with, went over there to check it out and the intruder bashed him on the head."

"Possibly," Mrs. Connors said. "But who could it have been? I can't imagine an employee of the school doing it. Who else could get in? The doors are locked and you have to be buzzed in."

"Yes, but people are pretty careless about it. You buzz one person in, somebody comes up behind them, and they hold the door open for that person too. Or people prop the door open while they carry in packages or supplies from their car, meanwhile anybody could slip in. Delivery men are in and out all the time. It's easier than you would think to get in."

"I suppose so, but it comes back to 'who?' and what would be the motive?"

"Ah, that's the sticking point, isn't it? I must confess I can't come up with a likely suspect, or figure out a motive," Mrs. DelMonte said. "I just hope the police solve it soon. It makes me nervous, realizing that there could be a murderer among us."

"Yes, I know what you mean," Mrs. Connors said. "I'm very uneasy, and I don't think the place will ever be the same."

Meg finished fiddling with her makeup which, truth be known, she hardly ever used, and exited the Ladies' Room and returned to the parlor. As she surveyed the scene, she saw Bob Glinski, the maintenance man, standing in a corner by himself and looking forlorn. As she moved toward him, she tried to think of what to say to start the conversation. Unable to think of a brilliant intro, she tried the old:

"Hi Bob, I'm glad you could come." She watched his reaction closely. She hoped that it didn't sound too artificial.

"I had to come and pay my respects, didn't I," he said mournfully.

Meg didn't know what to say next, so she thought she'd try the old "How do you think he looks?" 'Another stupid thing people say at Irish wakes,' she thought, 'but...that's where we are isn't it? When in Rome, do as the Romans do.'

"I haven't been up to the coffin," he said. "I can't stand to look at dead people. I saw too much of that, up close, in Afghanistan. I never go to wakes, but I felt I had to. I had to take a couple of Xanax to just get through walking in the door."

"Where did you get the Xanax, Bob," Meg asked. She knew it was one of the most common drugs traded and sold illegally on the street."

"I have a prescription for it from the VA Hospital."

"Oh, so you have anxiety disorder?" Meg asked.

"I'm being treated for PTSD at the VA. Service-related, from Afghanistan. I was planning on making a career of the Army, but I was wounded when an IED blew up right under my Humvee. I was one of the few survivors. I got a medical discharge and a disability pension. I go for counseling once a week at the VA."

Meg felt like a heel. "I'm sorry," she mumbled. "Thank you for your service." Glinski just nodded and grunted something under his breath.

Meg extracted herself and looked around for the next target. She saw Lester Nestorious standing near the wall and set sail in his direction.

"Hello Lester, very sad day isn't it?" She figured that would provoke something interesting.

"Umm," he grunted. 'I've got to get this conversation jump-started,' she thought.

"This is very tragic. I can't believe it. I knew him so well," she said. "I can't imagine who would do such a thing. What do you think, Lester?"

"Well, if I were you, I would start with the organist."

"Why do you say that?" Meg asked.

"Think about it. We know he quarreled with Deacon Tom shortly before his death. We know he was angry and promised to take it further. He's very temperamental and narcissistic. Got to have his own way all the time."

"But Lester, come on. Do you really think a quarrel over liturgical music is a motive for murder?"

"Not for a normal person, no. But Poole is high-strung, emotional and impulsive. He's very confrontational and he has to get his own way all the time. If he doesn't he broods and sulks. He's too full of himself by far. He doesn't react to little disagreements the way normal people do. He stews over them."

Meg thought for a moment, then she said: "OK, leaving the question of adequate motive aside for now, what was Bruce doing in the boiler room? What was Deacon Tom doing in the boiler room for that matter? Why would Bruce disconnect the gas supply from the boiler? And how and why did he get behind Deacon Tom to bash him in the head?"

Lester shrugged. "I don't know. That's what you're getting paid to figure out. Of course, if the audit shows that there's forty thousand dollars missing, then Rick Peters goes to the top of the list. But if the audit shows that Rick's explanation is correct, that it's all due to slow tuition collection, then Rick is out of the running, and my money is on Bruce Poole."

"Well, thanks Lester," she said. "You've given me some food for thought. I'll have to mull this over."

By this time viewing hours were over, and Meg and Joe made their exit from the funeral home. In the car on the way home, Joe said: "Well did you learn anything?"

"Nothing that we didn't already know," Meg said. "I'm more confused than ever, actually. I talked to a lot of people and got a lot of opinions. Some of them sounded crazy, but even though I know all of the potential suspects myself, it was interesting to hear other people's perspective on it. I'm going to have to think about this. How about you? What did you learn?"

"Same as you. I didn't learn any new facts, but I talked to a lot of people and got to know the actors better. And, as you said, their perspectives are interesting, even if some of them sounded crazy."

They said a long goodnight on Meg's front porch, and agreed to meet at the church at 9:30 in the morning for the funeral.

CHAPTER 19

WHEN MEG WALKED INTO THE CHURCH the next morning it was already almost two-thirds full. She found Joe waiting for her in the vestibule. "Grief becomes you," Joe said, noticing how elegant and simply well put together Meg looked in her tailored black dress. "Thank you," Meg blushed, grateful she had taken time to put up her hair and put on a little bit of makeup. "Let's split up," Joe said. "I'll sit in the last pew on the left, you sit halfway up on the right. That way we can keep the largest number of people under observation, watch what they do, who they interact with, etcetera." Meg was not keen on splitting up, but she realized that he was right. She walked up the right side aisle, found a seat in a pew about halfway up, genuflected, made the Sign of the Cross, and entered the pew.

As she looked around her, for some bizarre reason the movie "Casablanca" entered her mind. All the "usual suspects" were there. Rick Peters was seated on

one of the front pews on the right, next to Sister Moira
and a good deal of the faculty of the school. Becky and
Grace were on the other side, sitting together of course.
Bruce Poole was seated at the organ. The members of
the Parish Council seemed to have their own pew a
little further up on the left. 'I should actually be sitting with them, but I have to be able to observe everybody without attracting any attention,' she thought. Bob
Glinski was sitting by himself and looking lonely a few
pews in front of her.

The three pews in front on both sides had "Reserved"
signs on them and were empty. She knew that the ones
on the left were reserved for the deacons who vested in
alb, stole and dalmatic, and the ones on the right were
reserved for Tom's family. Two Deacons would be on
the altar, a Deacon of the Word and a Deacon of the
Eucharist, and the rest would sit in the reserved pews.

Suddenly the organ began to play "Be Not Afraid",
the procession entered the church and the congregation
rose. First came a tall altar boy in cassock and surplice,
bearing the cross and flanked on each side by altar boys
carrying lighted candles. Next came a long procession
of deacons, two-by-two, vested in white dalmatics, followed by about a dozen priests, vested in white chasu-
bles, and then Father Vince, who would be the main

celebrant. Following him came the casket, with six pall-bears, presumably relatives and friends of Tom, and finally, his wife and children, grandchildren and other family members.

The deacons took their seats on the left and the family on the right. Then Father Vince blessed the casket with holy water, placed a white pall and a cru-cifix on it, ascended the altar and began the Mass with the Sign of the Cross and the Opening Prayer. Tom's adult son, Matt, proclaimed the first reading, which was from 2 Maccabees 42, followed by Psalm 51 sung by the choir; then Tom's daughter, Brenda, proclaimed the Second reading from Revelations 21.

The Deacon of the Word stood up to proclaim the Gospel. Everyone rose, and he began to read the Gospel verse from Luke 10, about Jesus sending the Disciples out two-by-two. The words "Go, I am sending you out like lambs among wolves," struck Meg as somehow appropriate to the situation. Tom struck her as a great big fuzzy lamb. "Whoever listens to you, listens to me. Whoever rejects you, rejects me," the reading went on.

Father Vince gave the homily, and managed to tie the readings to Deacon Tom's ministry, his spirit of evangelization, his work in catechesis, his charity. He broke up several times during the homily, but pulled himself together with difficulty to continue. He ended by asking everyone to pray that the crime would be solved soon, and also to pray for the perpetrator.

Meg tried to keep the "usual suspects" in view and observe them during the homily. Becky and Grace cried at several points. Lester sat rigid and stony-faced. His sidekicks fidgeted. Sister Moira also cried, and Rick Peters, sitting next to her, patted her hand and looked very uncomfortable. Bob Glinski looked as white as a sheet. Bruce Poole was sitting at the organ, also fidgeting and squirming in his seat. Meg thought to herself, 'this is one of those rare moments when a homily does what it's supposed to do: make everybody uncomfortable.'

The rest of the Mass proceeded normally. At communion time, nearly the entire congregation went to communion, but Meg noted that Bruce Poole, Bob Glinski and Lester Nestorious all remained in their seats. She refrained from drawing any conclusions about that, because she knew that there could be many different reasons for it.

After the funeral, the whole congregation and clergy, led by a bagpiper in kilt and tartan, processed with the casket to Holy Cross Cemetery, two blocks away, led and followed by police motorcycles. After the usual graveside prayers, Tom's body was interred, and the congregation quietly dispersed, all going their separate ways in silence.

Meg and Joe walked the two blocks back to the Church, where they retrieved the police car Joe came in. As they walked, they exchanged their observations about the various characters, their behavior and their demeanor. But in the end, they agreed that they couldn't draw any useful conclusion from what they had seen and observed. It was all pretty normal behavior at a funeral.

Back in the car, Joe said, " So we're no further along than we were before, is that the takeaway from this morning?"

"I guess so," Meg said. "Nobody behaved in an unusual way. There was nothing that made me suspect one of them more than another."

"Well, let's grab some lunch first, then go back to the station house, get our notes together, and meet with the Inspector," Joe said.

"Sounds like a plan," Meg said. Maybe he'll have some suggestions or directions for us.

CHAPTER 20

BACK AT THE STATION HOUSE, MEG AND
Joe reviewed their notes, tried to organize them and
to make some sense of them. They had recorded their
interviews with the various principals and witnesses,
and a police report technician had transcribed them.
They reviewed the transcripts to refresh their recollec-
tion. They made three sets of copies of everything, and
put them in three loose-leaf binders, one for each of
them, and one for the Inspector. They spent a couple of
hours at this, and then they decided they were ready for
a case conference with the Inspector.

Inspector Flanagan met with them in the station
house conference room. They gave him one of the
loose-leaf binders, and an oral precis of all of the interviews and other evidence they had gathered. As they
were finishing their oral report, there was a knock on
the conference room door, and the Desk Lieutenant
came into the room. "Excuse me, Inspector, but this

was just hand-delivered for you. I thought you'd want to see it right away." He handed the Inspector a Manila envelope. Inspector Flanagan opened the envelope, and removed a double-spaced typed report, about six pages long. He glanced at it and let out a sigh.

"This is what we've all been waiting for," he said. "It's the report from the accounting firm on the school audit. I'm going to make two copies of this, and we're all going to read it together. This should determine one way or another where we're going with this investigation."

As he left to make the copies, Meg and Joe looked at each other with nervous anticipation. "This is like waiting for the envelope to be opened at the Academy Awards," Joe quipped. "Yes it is," Meg said. "But nobody's going to win a prize. Somebody might be in big trouble though."

The Inspector came back after a few minutes and handed each of them a copy of the report. They all read it in silence, going over each page and each chart and column of figures very carefully, taking their time. When they finished, they looked at each other and all let out a collective sigh of relief.

"Well," the Inspector said, "the bottom line is that there is no money missing. The explanation that the Assistant Principal has been giving all along is correct.

It's solely a cash-flow problem, due to slow tuition collection coupled with some unanticipated expenditures. It's exactly what he's been saying all along, so it looks like he's in the clear."

Meg sighed. "I'm very relieved, and happy for him," she said. "I never thought he would steal money from the school, let alone that he would kill Deacon Tom. The whole idea was totally unfathomable to me."

"True," Joe said. "I never fancied him as a thief or a killer either, but it leaves us with nobody with a credible motive. Where do we go from here?"

After a pause, the Inspector said: "You know, it strikes me that this is a very odd case. We all know that the three critical factors in solving any crime are: "means, opportunity and motive. Most of the time, we're looking for means and opportunity. But in this case," he continued, "means and opportunity are everywhere. The means was a monkey wrench that was laying on the boiler room floor for anybody to pick up. And opportunity? There were a couple of dozen adults in the school, counting all the teachers, cafeteria workers, staff and the two women selling SCRIP. They all had opportunity, at least theoretically.

"And then there's the other suspects we've been considering," he continued. "Like the other parish council members. Although the office secretary doesn't remember buzzing any of them in that day, we've established that everybody was lax about propping the door open, holding the door open for others to enter, etcetera. All of the parish council members had a right to be there. Nobody would have thought anything odd about them following somebody in or entering when the door was propped open. So, the bottom line is that the means was there for anybody's use, and everybody had opportunity."

"So, are we back to square one? How do we proceed?" Meg asked. She wanted badly to solve the case because of her affection for Deacon Tom. But, she also wasn't in a hurry to go back to uniformed patrol.

They all looked at each other in puzzlement. "Any suggestions?" the Inspector said.

"Well, why don't we do what Agatha Christie would do?" Meg said.

The Inspector laughed, and Joe looked at her quizzically. "And what would Agatha Christie do?" the Inspector asked.

"She would have Hercule Poirot make a list of all of the suspects, and after each name list the things that either implicate or exonerate him or her. Then Poirot would start eliminating people. At the end, he would either have a very small list, or he might even have the perp as the only man standing."

The Inspector raised his eyebrows. "O.K., let's do it," he said. "You make the list, Meg," he directed. The Inspector got up, went to a cupboard, took out a yellow lined pad, and tossed it to her.

"Everybody?" she asked. He thought for a minute. "Yes, everybody. Some we will eliminate quickly, but let's start with everybody. They have to work their way off the list, not on it." Meg began to write. When she finished, she got up, went to the copier, made two copies and gave them to the Inspector and to Joe. The list was as follows:

Sister Moira

Rick Peters

Father Vince

Bruce Poole

Marty O'Connor

Bob Glinski

Grace O'Neill

Becky Nowak

Lester Nestorious

Judge Sadowski

Joe Browne

Jim Curran

O.K., the Inspector said, we evaluate every one as to means, opportunity and motive. Only if we find that a suspect had all three, do we begin to discuss how likely he or she is.

"Don't you think this is very much a male crime, Inspector?" Joe asked. "Women usually don't bash people over the head with a blunt instrument."

"Statistically, you're right," the Inspector said. "But we don't start out excluding anybody. We consider everybody until we find a reason to exclude them."

"Right," he said. "Let's begin. Sister Moira. Any comments?"

"Obviously, she had means and opportunity," Meg said. "She's the principal, She has keys to every door. But no motive. She thought the world of Deacon Tom. Besides, she's a gentle little old lady. She doesn't even like to swat flies. She opens the window and shoos them out."

"Right. Scratch Sister Moira," the Inspector said. "Next, Father Vince."

"Ditto, with Sister Moira," Joe said. "He had means and opportunity. He also has keys to everything. And unlike Sister Moira, he knows what a monkey wrench looks like. But no motive. He was very fond of Deacon Tom. Tom was his right hand."

"Scratch Father Vince. How about Rick Peters? We've eliminated the financial motive, but what else do we know about him?"

"We've checked him thoroughly, Chief," Joe said. "Glowing recommendations from the other schools where he taught, ditto from his grad school professors, no rap sheet of any kind, passed the background check required for all school administrators. We didn't find a single strike against him."

"Scratch him. How about Bruce Poole?"

Meg and Joe looked at each other. Joe signaled Meg to go ahead. "We don't have anything specific on him Chief. But we both think he's not playing with a full deck. In layman's terms, he's the type that might explode some day."

"Elaborate," the Inspector said.

"He's very narcissistic," Meg said. "He's totally wrapped up in his own world. He can't see anything but his own concerns. He has no sense of proportion. He doesn't like to be crossed, he has a short fuse, and he carries a grudge. A lot of this information is from my experience with him on the Parish Council. I've just seen him throw too many hissy fits. I'm not saying he's a murderer, but I am saying I think he's unstable, and I don't like to be around him when he loses it."

Joe nodded. "I don't know him like Meg does, but that is pretty much the book that I've picked up on him as well," he said.

"Okay, Poole stays on the list, near the top. We'll have to poke around his background some more," the Inspector said. "Also, look for some motive other than that disagreement over liturgical music. I don't fancy that as a motive for murder."

"Next, Marty O'Connor," Flanagan read.

"I think he's a scratch," Meg said. "He's President of the Parish Council, he liked and admired Deacon Tom, and he was working in City Hall at the time of the crime."

The Inspector drew a line through his name. "Scratch," he said.

"Next, Bob Glinski," the Inspector read from the list.

"Clearly, means and opportunity," Meg said. "As maintenance man, he had keys to everything, and spent quite of bit of time in the boiler room. Also, he knew where all the tools were kept. But we can't find a motive. Father Vince gave him this job when he got out of the military, and he seems to love it. He is very competent, but very quiet. Never bothers anybody. We were unable to find any complaints about him."

"What did he do in the military?" the Inspector asked.

"He was in the Army and served in Afghanistan," Meg said. "He got wounded when an IED blew up under his Humvee. Some of his buddies were killed. He got a disability retirement."

"What is the disability?" the Inspector asked.

"I don't know exactly," Meg said. "But I know he's treating at the VA Hospital for PTSD. He told me that."

"Okay, no motive, but he stays on the list for now. We need to find out more about him."

"Next, Grace O'Neill," the Inspector said.

"We might as well take Grace and Becky together," Meg said. "They're like Frick and Frack. They're always together. No motive, not means, no opportunity. They were in the building at the time. In fact they sounded the alarm when they smelled gas, but they were in plain view right in front of the cafeteria door the whole time. Lots of people saw them. They both have small children in the school. I think we can eliminate them."

"Agreed," the Inspector said. "Okay, Lester Nestorious. Tell me about him."

"Lester is a grumpy old malcontent," Meg said. "He's always complaining about something. He has really weird views. But didn't have motive, means or opportunity. He never goes near the school, he doesn't have any keys. He's always arguing with everybody, but it's just general crankiness. Nobody takes him very seriously. He had no particular problem with Deacon Tom, other than irritation that Tom wouldn't fire Bruce Poole. But that wasn't Tom's call."

"When you say 'weird views,' what do you mean?" the Inspector asked.

"Oh, for example he thinks the Pope is a heretic. He thinks there has been no legitimate Pope since Pius X who died in 1914."

"Interesting. So in other words, he's a nut."

"Well, I would rather say he's eccentric. He definitely has odd theological views, but I don't see him as a murderer. And he didn't have means or opportunity, and I can't see any motive."

"Well, keep him on the list because he's a crank, and cranks can be unpredictable. But he's not a high priority. I agree nothing points to him at the moment. "

"I think we can say the same for the next three, Inspector. Judge Sadowski, Joe Browne and Jim Curran. They're part of Lester's 'caucus' you might say, whom the British would call 'bacbenchers.' They gripe and complain and tend to be against the way things are going in the Church, but they didn't have means or opportunity, never go near the school, and didn't have anything against Deacon Tom," Meg reported confidently.

"Okay, scratch them," the inspector replied, " but in pencil, and keep your eyes and ears open. You may still pick up new information."

"So where are we?" Joe asked.

"Where we are is that we have two suspects who need further investigation," the inspector stated. "Joe, I want you to look into Bruce Poole. Talk to his former employers, his neighbors, find out where he hangs out, talk to his former professors, get all the scoop you can on him."

"Right Chief," Joe said.

"Meg, I want you to go to the VA Hospital, talk to Glinski's psychologist or whoever he sees there, and see what you can find out that could be helpful about him."

"Okay Chief," she said. "But they're going to hide behind HIPPA regulations and refuse to tell me anything."

"I know, but see what you can do. Mention the word 'subpoena' a few times. Don't actually threaten a sub-poena, but you can mention that we are gathering evi-dence for a Grand Jury presentation, which is true, and that a Grand Jury can issue a subpoena which trumps

HIPPA regulations. Mention to the therapist that you certainly wouldn't want to compel him or her to testify before a Grand Jury if it can be helped. See if that doesn't help the therapist remember some useful things that are outside the scope of HIPPA."

"Right, Chief," she said.

"Okay, that was a good day's work. You both have you work cut out for you tomorrow. Get some rest tonight."

CHAPTER 21

THE NEXT DAY MEG DROVE ACROSS town to the VA Hospital. After bouncing around from bureaucrat to bureaucrat, she finally found herself seated in a comfortable office facing a female psychologist across the table. Dr. Margaret Cooley was 40ish, short and sort of stocky, with jet black hair cut in a bob, an ivory complexion and large, clear blue eyes. She was wearing a conservatively cut blue business suit, with a white silk blouse. The sign on her desk said: "Dr. Margaret Cooley, B.A., M.S., Ph.D., Staff Psychologist." The diplomas on the wall revealed that her B.A. and M.A. were from Fordham University, and her Ph.D. was from NYU. 'Impressive credentials,' Meg thought. 'Expensive schools. Either she come from a well-to-do family, or she won a lot of scholarships.'

Meg presented her credentials and explained the purpose of her visit.

"We're investigating a homicide, Dr. Cooley," she said. "You've probably read about it in the papers or have seen it on television. A clergyman was struck on the head with a blunt instrument in an elementary school boiler room, and then left to die from carbon monoxide poisoning."

The doctor showed no expression and looked at Meg impassively. "Yes, I have read about it," she said. "But I don't see what it has to do with me."

"Well," Meg said, "We have to consider everyone who was on the premises at the time and potentially had access to the boiler room as a possible suspect. This is standard procedure. We have to look into not only their whereabouts at the time, but also their background."

"Yes?' the doctor asked.

"Well, one of the employees of the school, a mainte-nance man who had access to the boiler room and in fact had more access than anybody else to the entire prem-ises, is a man named Bob Glinski. I have interviewed him and he has told me that he is being treated here for service-connected PTSD. The Assistant Administrator of the Hospital told me that you are his therapist. I need all the information I can get on Bob Glinski to for a full picture. That's why I'm here."

Dr. Cooley stared at Meg, still impassive.

"I see," she said. "Well surely you understand that HIPPA Regulations prohibit me from revealing any details about a patient."

Meg maintained eye-contact and pressed on. "Yes, I assure you I fully understand HIPPA Regulations," she replied. "But you have to understand that this is a murder investigation. We are preparing to present this case to the Grand Jury. A Grand Jury has subpoena power, and its subpoena trumps HIPPA Regulations. And the Grand Jury can not only subpoena patient records, but it can also subpoena a treating provider to testify. We would like to spare you that, so all I'm asking is that you give me any information that you can, within professional ethics, that may help us in this investigation."

The doctor's icy composure was broken by a tiny, almost imperceptible shudder, but she maintained her otherwise stolid composure.

"I have never testified before a Grand Jury, and I'm not anxious to have the experience," she said with a frown. "But I can't reveal information given to me confidentially by a patient in treatment. I will have to consult with the hospital's attorney."

Meg knew where that was going to go. Nowhere. Then she had an idea.

"Look," she said. "Let's keep this more informal for the time being. How about if I ask you some hypothetical, generic questions about PTSD, and you give me some hypothetical, generic answers, with the understanding that we are not talking about any specific patient?"

Dr. Cooley pondered that suggestion for a moment. Apparently realizing that Meg was not going to go away and drop the matter, she apparently decided the suggestion might be an acceptable way out of a sticky situation.

"All right, we'll give it a try," she said. "If I see that we're wandering into forbidden territory, I'll stop, but for the time being, we'll give it a try."

"Very good," Meg said. "First of all, what is PTSD? How is it defined and what does it consist of?"

"PTSD stands for Post Traumatic Stress Disorder," she said. "It is caused by experiencing, either as a participant or as a witness, a severe trauma or a life-threatening event. Something out of the ordinary, beyond everyday experience, something that would not normally be expected in our regular environment. For example, if you were involved in a minor fender-bending accident with no injuries, it would not be expected to cause PTSD. But if you involved in, or witnessed, a fatal accident, especial if you saw the mangled, bloody bodies, and so on, that would be expected to cause PTSD."

"What are the symptoms?" Meg asked.

"There are many symptoms. Some of them are a feeling of anxiety, being constantly on edge. Sudden noises make you jumpy, provoke a more severe reaction than normal. Recurring nightmares are a big symptom. You keep reliving the traumatic event in you nightmares, over and over. You become withdrawn, don't socialize with people. Don't go out of your house any more than you have to. You may have trouble sleeping. You lose interest in the normal things of daily life that used to give you pleasure."

"Other symptoms include a feeling of numbness," she continued. "You don't react to emotional events, either good or bad, that other people would normally react to. Anger and irritability are big symptoms. Ordinary things that wouldn't disturb most people cause you to erupt with anger or an emotional outburst. Another one is a feeling of being constantly on guard, of expecting something awful to happen when there is no reason to. These symptoms don't have to all be present, but there are among the big ones that often are."

"Do you see much PTSD from Afghanistan?" Meg asked.

"Oh yes. A ton of it. Afghanistan and Iraq. It accounts for probably three-quarters of my patient load. Mine and the three other psychologists on the staff here."

"Wow. I didn't realize it was so prevalent," Meg said.

The doctor was warming to her subject now. This was a home game.

"Yes, most people don't realize." she said. "It's a silent killer. Afghanistan is our nation's longest wars. And it was very unconventional. Most of the soldiers who were killed were not killed in a conventional battle. They were killed by roadside bombs, IED's. Some were killed in their sleep when the Taliban or ISIS blew up a barracks or set of a bomb in a hotel or restaurant. Some of them were killed by Afghani soldiers or policemen who were being trained by American trainers, and who opened fire on their comrades and the American trainers, killing dozens. Oh yes. All war is hell but the war in off a roadside bomb. Afghanistan has been a particularly gruesome one, resulting in a lot of PTSD in the returning veterans. It's far more common than anyone realizes."

"That's awful," Meg said.

"Yes, and what makes it worse is that when they come home, they do not get the recognition and the empathy that they deserve and need. Afghanistan is a forgotten war. Unless you have a loved one over there, you probably don't think about it at all."

"How do you deal with it yourself?" Meg asked.

"With great difficulty. You want to, and need to, show empathy. And yet, you also have to maintain a professional detachment. We don't see a lot of success. There's no cure for it. In the best case scenario, it can be treated and more or less managed, but there's no permanent cure. Relapses are common. You can give the patients strategies and tools, but they're not guarantees. If a "blackout" occurs, there's no use saying 'you shouldn't have done that.' They weren't aware of what they were doing at the time. They saw themselves back in Kabul in a burning barracks, or whatever," the doctor replied.

"Interesting," Meg said. She pauses for a moment and mulled something over in her mind.

"This sort of brings us to the heart of the matter," she said. "Can I present you with a hypothetical situation and ask you what you would think of that situation?"

"Yes," Dr. Cooley said. "This is commonly what we are asked to do in court. When we are called to testify as an expert witness, we are given a hypothetical, and asked to give our opinion on the hypothetical."

"Okay. So here's the hypothetical," Meg said. "Suppose a veteran, suffering from diagnosed PTSD, were in a confined space, say a boiler room, in let's say a crouching or kneeling position working on repairs or adjustments to a boiler which required intense concentration. Now suppose someone came up behind him and startled him with a sudden noise or something, and at that moment the veteran had a flashback. In his mind he was back in Afghanistan in an ambush or whatever traumatic event gave rise to the PTSD in the first place, and he lashed out and struck the person who startled him with a blunt instrument which he had, maybe in his hand or close at hand. Are those facts reasonable?"

Dr. Cooley paused thoughtfully and replied, "Yes, they are and yes I have the hypothetical."

Meg leaned in, saying, "Good. So then in that case, in your professional opinion, would that vet realize what he was doing, and would he be responsible for what he did?'

Dr Cooley smiled. "You should be a lawyer. You sound like you've done this before," she said.

"I haven't done it before, but I've seen it done before," Meg replied.

"Given those hypothetical facts, in that case it would be like sleepwalking," Dr. Cooley said. "That person would not realize what he was doing, and therefore would not be responsible for what he was doing. And he also may not remember it afterwards."

"Thank you very much, Dr. Cooley," Meg said.

"Have I been of any help?" the doctor asked.

"You've been very helpful. When I came in to your office, I didn't know where this case was going. Now I think I know."

"Will I be called to testify?" Dr. Cooley asked.

"Possibly. But maybe not. It might not be necessary," Meg said.

CHAPTER 22

LATER THAT AFTERNOON, MEG AND JOE met back at the station house, in the Inspectors office, to review and compare their findings. After they each got a cup of police station coffee, the thickness of motor oil and about as tasty, they settled in to give their reports.

"You go first, Joe," the Inspector said.

"Chief, I talked to the pastors at the previous parishes where Poole worked, as well as some of the people he worked with, cantors, liturgy committee members, and so forth.

"They all tell pretty much the same story. The book on Poole is that he's cranky, ornery, touchy, loves to start drama and act offended, complains about everything. But I couldn't find any evidence that he was ever violent. His acting out is all verbal. He has no rap sheet, and I couldn't find anything that would constitute a motive. He argued with Deacon Tom over the music group as we know, but nobody thinks that was very serious, and certainly not a motive for murder."

"So," Joe continued, "the bottom line is that Poole is not somebody you'd want to share a foxhole with, but there's absolutely nothing to suggest him as a likely suspect for murder, and nothing to suggest a motive for killing Deacon Tom."

The Inspector looked at Meg. "Any comment on that, Meg?" he asked.

"No sir, that's pretty much what I expected. It's consistent with my experience with Poole."

"All right. I'm not going to completely eliminate him from the list, but unless a motive that we don't know about now turns up, he goes to the bottom."

He turned to Meg. "Okay Meg, your turn. Did you come up with anything at the VA?"

"Yes sir, I think I did. In fact, I think I know how it happened. I haven't got all the details yet, but I think I see a general outline of what happened and how it happened."

"Really? All right, we're all ears. Tell us about it."

Meg took a deep breath. This was her big chance. If she was right, it could result in the gold badge of a detective. If she wasn't right, she'd look like a fool, and it'd be back to driving up and down the streets in a black and white ten hours a day.

"Well," she began, "I met with Dr. Margaret Cooley, Bob Glinski's treating psychologist at the VA Hospital. At first of course, she cited HIPPA regulations and refused to tell me anything, but I mentioned the words 'subpoena' and 'Grand Jury' a few times, not threatening of course, but just pointing out this case will be presented to a Grand jury and they can issue subpoenas of medical records and even compel testimony. After having dropped that hint, we discussed her dilemma some more and worked out a procedure where we would discuss a 'hypothetical' case, and she would tell me her professional opinion of what would take place in that hypothetical case. She agreed to that, and I think it was very fruitful. I think she managed to tell me some things without telling me, if you know what I mean."

Joe was looking at here with approval, and sitting on the edge of his chair.

"Very good, you have our attention. Tell us what you found out," the Inspector said.

"Well, first of all, Dr. Cooley explained PTSD to me. PTSD results from participating in or observing a very traumatic event, such as a fatal accident, or participating in a battle in war time, especially a battle in which you witness people being killed or maimed, or maybe, but not necessarily, being seriously wounded yourself. What happened to Glinski, his squad was driving down a road and the Taliban detonated an IED under their Humvee, wounding Glinski and killing three of his comrades, is a classic case. He was hospitalized for quite a while, and his three buddies were killed instantly. Among other things, he suffers from 'survivor's guilt.' He feels tremendous guilt that he's still alive and his buddies are not."

"The symptoms of PTSD are hyper-vigilance, constantly feeling on edge, withdrawal from socialization and from the normal pleasures of life, agitation, irritability, sleeplessness, nightmares, reacting violently to sudden, startling noises, severe anxiety, emotional detachment, unwanted thoughts, flashbacks and blackouts.

"Flashbacks mean you relive the traumatic event that caused the PTSD as if it were happening for the first time. It's like you're sleepwalking. You could be sitting in Starbuck's having coffee, and you have a flashback and you think you're back in Kabul being ambushed by the enemy. Blackouts mean you aren't aware of what's going on and may not remember it later."

Meg took a breath. "Are you with me so far?" she asked.

Joe and the Inspector were both listening with rapt attention.

"Keep those symptoms in mind, because some of them are going to be key components of what I think happened here."

"So what do you think happened?" the Inspector asked.

"I suggest that the reason we can't find a suspect with a motive, is because there is no suspect with a motive. I think what happened is that Bob Glinski was in the boiler room, doing some kind of work on the boiler. This would not be unusual. Part of his job is maintaining the boiler. I think that, for whatever reason, Deacon Tom entered the boiler room, inadvertently startled Bob, who had a flashback, lashed out with whatever tool he had in his hand, and hit Deacon Tom."

"Okay, let's accept this as a hypothesis for the moment. But that doesn't explain why and how the gas feed got disconnected," Inspector Flanagan said.

"I know," Meg said. "I'm convinced this is the general outline of what happened. But the only way we're going to find out the details is to question Bob and get him to tell us. If he even remembers, and he may not."

The Inspector got up and paced the room, clasping his hands behind his back and frowning. Meg and Joe looked at each other. They were both quietly wondering, 'What do we do next?'

Finally the Inspector stopped pacing and said, "I can see that this situation raises all kinds of problems and questions that are above our pay grades. Can we question him? Given our suspicions about his mental health, should we have a psychologist or psychiatrist present? Should we seek a forensic mental health exam? How would we go about doing that? Normally, the judge does that at arraignment upon the request of either attorney or on his own authority if he sees reason to question the defendant's mental health. But I am nowhere near arresting this guy, so there isn't going to be an arraignment anytime soon, so how would we get him a forensic psych exam? Do we have the authority?

"Right now, we do not have probable cause to make an arrest," he continued. ""All we have at present is intuition. Don't get me wrong Meg, I think I agree with your intuition. But we can't make an arrest based on it. If your theory of the case is correct, Meg, there were only two people present when this thing went down, and one of them is dead and the other one is nuts. So where are we going with this?"

"With all due respect, sir," Meg said, "I wouldn't say he's 'nuts.' He's mentally ill, but competent enough to tell us what happened, if he remembers. If he had a total blackout, he may not remember anything, but on the other hand he may remember some or all of it."

"Yes, but how do we get him to talk to us?" Joe asked. "If we just invite him in for a chat, he may tell us to take a hike. Or, given his PTSD, he may get spooked and do a bunk. Or worse. God forbid, he may off himself. On the other hand, if we pick him up, it's a custodial interrogation and we have to read him his Miranda rights. Then he'll probably 'lawyer-up,' and his lawyer won't let him answer any questions."

Meg looked crestfallen. "You're right, Joe, so what can we do?"

"I'll tell you what we can do," Flanagan said. "There are advantages to not being the top dog. We kick this baby upstairs. I'm going to go see the Commissioner, and ask him to set up a meeting with the District Attorney. I'll dump it in his lap. He will have to tell us how to proceed from here on."

"So we just sit tight and wait to hear from you, Chief?" Joe asked.

"Right," the Inspector said. "Review your notes, write up your reports, and email them to me as soon as they're ready, but don't do anything else until further notice. I'll try to schedule a meeting with the D.A. for tomorrow."

CHAPTER 23

LATE THE NEXT AFTERNOON, MEG AND Joe found themselves sitting in the large and rather ornate office of the District Attorney, John M. Farley, along with the Commissioner of Police, Peter J. Broderick, and Inspector Flanagan. They were seated in leather armchairs, surrounded by walls covered with oak paneling. On the left, the wall was lined with built-in bookcases filled with volumes of legal books. On the right, the wall was covered with pictures, mainly of D.A. Farley with various important politicians, including the President, two Governors, the Mayor, and various other dignitaries. There was a picture, obviously taken in Rome, of Farley, flanked by his wife in a black dress and black mantilla, in a line of people shaking hands with the Pope.

To say that Meg was intimidated would be an understatement. Her stomach was in knots. Her pulse was racing. She made a silent mental prayer: 'Please God, don't let me be wrong about this. Don't let me make a fool of myself."

The Commissioner introduced her, gave her the floor and asked her to explain to the D.A. what conclusion she had come to, how she had reached it, and what her reasons were. Meg gave an accurate but brief precis of the crime and the entire investigation. She explained how they were stymied because they couldn't find a suspect with a motive. Then she explained that, one day she was thinking about it, and the thought came to her that maybe they couldn't find a motive because there wasn't any. What if nobody had deliberately killed Deacon Tom? What if the whole thing were some sort of an accident?

She went over the story of Bob Glinski being wounded in Afghanistan and witnessing his buddies being blown to bits before his eyes, his long recovery, his survivors' guilt, his being diagnosed with Post Traumatic Stress Disorder. She went over her interview with Dr. Cooley at the VA Hospital, her explanation of PTSD, its symptoms and effects, and the hypothetical question she put to Dr. Cooley and the doctor's answer. When she had finished she exhaled a big sigh of relief. She felt like an actor who had just finished her debut on the big stage. She paused and waited for a reaction.

All eyes were on Farley, who was widely-known as a tough, experienced, no-nonsense D.A.

Farley, in a dark suit with a blue and gold school tie, was sitting with his elbows on his desk, his forearms forming a tent, his fingertips as the peak. There was a pause while everybody seemed to be holding their breath. Finally he spoke.

"That was very well and succinctly put," he said. "You handled the interview with the psychologist well, and summarized it well. You phrased the hypothetical question exactly the way we do it in court. If you ever decide to go to law school, I could use you on this side of the street."

Meg felt herself blushing. "Thank you sir," she said.

"I supposed you're here because you don't know what to do next?" he said.

"Exactly," the Commissioner said. "To say that this case is unique would be an understatement. I've never run into anything quite like it."

"It's not common, that's for sure," Farley said.

"If it happened the way Officer Ryan thinks it did, and I find her theory of the case quite plausible, and more likely than anything else we've got, then it's not murder. There's no criminal intent. The most it might be is involuntary manslaughter, and that might be a stretch. The jury might not buy it."

"Might not even get that far. The Grand Jury might not indict. Although Grand Juries usually follow the advice of the D.A., I wouldn't bet the farm on this one. For that matter, I'm not at all sure I would push for an indictment on this one. I don't mind telling you I'd lose some sleep over it. I was a young lieutenant, one year out of Notre Dame, when I found myself a platoon leader in Vietnam. I still have nightmares about what I saw over there. No, if it happened the way you think it happened, I don't fancy this case at all."

"Well, unfortunately, the only way to find out is to get him to tell us. If it went down the way we think it did, the only other person who was there is dead, and there were no witnesses," Meg said.

"Right," Farley said.

The Commissioner said, "Our questions for you are: Do we question him? Can we question him, given that we have doubts about his mental status? Do we Mirandize him? Do we have to have a psychiatrist present? I don't think we have enough evidence to have him committed. We've already questioned him once, and he seemed normal, if withdrawn."

"Yes, I see the dilemma." Farley paused for a moment before continuing. "The case presents a number of fine points of Fifth and Sixth Amendment law."

He paused further, seeming to turn the options over in his mind as he played with a letter-opener on his desk. Finally, he seemed to come to a decision.

"First of all, we don't take him into custody," he said. "We don't have sufficient grounds. We only have a theory. So, we invite him in for a chat with us. If he's not in custody, you don't have to Mirandize him. You explain to him that he's not in custody, and he's free to leave. It's risky. He may do so, and then we're up the creek without a paddle. But somehow, I don't think he will. If he remembers what happened, he may even want to get it off his chest.

"We don't do it in a normal interrogation room, with a steel table and two steel chairs bolted to the floor. We use a comfortable room with leather armchairs and a coffee table and end tables, like a living room. We have a one-way mirror. I'll be behind the mirror, with a one of our consultant psychiatrists as observers."

"How do we get him in?" the Commissioner asked.

"Ryan, you have a relationship of sorts with him. He knows you and is apparently at ease with you, at least as much as he is with anybody. You simply call him up and ask him to come and have a chat with you," the DA replied. "Tell him you need his help tying up some loose ends. Of course, he's free to refuse, but as I said, I don't think he will. Does that sound like a plan?"

Meg and Joe looked at each other and nodded.

"Yes, I think it does," the Commissioner said. "It may very well work, and in any case, we're out of options. We have nothing to lose by trying it."

There seemed to be a collective sigh of agreement in the room.

"Any questions?" Farley asked.

"Just one," Joe said. "When we tell him he has a right to a lawyer, what if he says he wants one?"

"Then we get him one," the D.A. said. "We tell him he can call whoever he wants if he has a lawyer, if he says he doesn't have one and can't afford one, we get him Assigned Counsel. It may complicate things a little bit, but maybe not. A good lawyer would see that we may not have a criminal case because of lack of *mens rea,* so it's to his advantage to cooperate with us."

"Sounds like a plan," the Commissioner said.

"Good," said Farley. "I'll arrange for a suitable room in this building. A comfortable meeting room, that doesn't look like a police interrogation room. Ryan, you reach out to Glinski and tell him you need his help tying up some loose ends, and you'd like to meet with him and see if he can help you. Put it to him that way. Low key. Talk to him like a fellow parishioner, not like a copper. Needless to say, no uniform. Don't dress like a detective either. No visible gun, cuffs or badge. If you don't mind, dress very feminine. Approach it like a sister, solicitous for his feelings, etcetera. We'll be right behind the one-way mirror. Don't worry, you'll be well-covered."

"Just out of curiosity, sir, will I be alone with him?"

Farley looked around the room. "What do you guys think?" he asked. "Ryan alone, or Ryan and Curran together?"

Meg, Joe and the Commissioner all looked at each other. There was a moment of silence. Then Meg spoke up.

"With all due respect, sir, I think he will be more at ease with me alone."

"I agree," said the Commissioner. "We'll be right the other side of the mirror. We'll be in the room in a flash if anything goes south."

Joe nodded agreement.

"Right then," Farley said. "Give me a day, then you give him a call and set a time, and I'll make all the other arrangements.

CHAPTER 24

LATE THE NEXT AFTERNOON MEG FOUND herself sitting in a room on the sixth floor of the county office building. The room was furnished like a living room in a house just as the DA had described. There was grey carpeting on the floor and three deep, brown, leather armchairs. Two of the walls were painted green. The third had a large mirror in the middle of the wall, with floor-length bookcases on both sides, filled with leather bound books. The fourth wall contained the door. Meg was dressed in a black, knee-length A-line skirt, black pumps, and a soft, mauve colored sweater. She was occupying one of the armchairs, trying hard not to be nervous, as she waited for Bob Glinski to arrive. She found that her mind was racing a hundred miles an hour. She was as jittery as a cat on a hot tin roof. A great deal depended on her not screwing this up. She tried mentally reciting the *Memorare,* and found that concentrating on remembering the words took her mind off her immediate stress. Soon, she felt composed and much more confident in her abilities, not to mention those of the crew on the other side of the two way mirror.

Shortly there was a knock on the door, it opened, and a secretary showed Bob Glinski into the room. Meg rose, greeted him, and invited him to sit in the armchair to her right.

"Thank you for coming, Bob," she said. She crossed her legs and folded her hands in her lap. 'Non-threatening body language,' she told herself. "I really appreciate you coming and helping me out with a few points, but before we start, I want to be sure you understand that you're not obligated to be here, and you're free to leave any time you want. You're also free to have an attorney here if you wish."

She held her breath and waited for his reply.

"No, I trust you, Meg," he said. "And I don't like lawyers, so I'd rather just talk to you. I've known you a few years, and I think you're a very kind person."

Meg exhaled a silent sigh of relief, but at the same time felt a pang of guilt, as if she were somehow taking advantage of him. 'Don't be silly,' she told herself, 'if he says what I think he's going to say, this will all work out for the best in the end.'

She had rehearsed this moment over and over in her mind. She had decided, after much agonizing thought, and after discussing it with Joe and the Inspector, that the best way to approach it was to jump right in with both feet.

"Bob," she began, "I'm trying to piece together what happened that day. I think I know pretty much, but I need your help with some of the details. You were there in the boiler room that day, weren't you Bob?"

He sat there silently for what seemed to her an eternity, his face expressionless, just staring at her. The seconds ticked away. She thought 'what am I going to do if he doesn't answer me?' Her stomach turned over. It was probably only two or three minutes, but it seemed to her to be hours.

Finally he answered her. "What makes you think that?" he said.

"All the circumstantial evidence points to it. It's the only thing that makes any sense. I'm not trying to ambush you Bob. Really I'm not. I'm trying to help you. If it happened the way I think it happened, you'll be alright."

Silence. He still sat there, stony faced, looking down at the carpet. 'I have to jump-start this somehow,' she thought.

"You liked Deacon Tom, didn't you Bob," she said gently.

He looked up and made eye contact, with a pleading look on his face. He started to tremble. His voice faltered.

'We've broken the ice,' Meg thought to herself.

"Yes, I did," he said pleadingly. "I really did. I never meant to hurt him. It was an accident. He startled me, and I had a flashback. It was as if I was back in Afghanistan. I didn't even know where I was. All I knew was that I was being ambushed again, and I lashed out."

"Tell me exactly what happened," she said softly.

"The school boiler was on the blink. It wasn't functioning properly. I was in a stew about it. I knew the school and the parish were in financial difficulties. Everybody was talking about it, everybody was worried. I knew that the school almost wasn't able to meet the teacher payroll recently."

His voice was faltering and he was trembling.

"Take your time," Meg said.

"I know that boiler is old, and won't last much longer. And I also know that the parish couldn't afford to replace it right now. I didn't want to cause Father Vince any more worry than he already has." He looked up and made eye contact again. "Father Vince has been so good to me. He gave me a job when I needed one badly. He helped get me hooked up with the VA for treatment and counseling. He has spent a lot of time counseling me, trying to get me over the bumps.

"So, I was trying to repair the boiler, to coax some more life out of it. Make it last a few more years. There was something wrong with the gas feed, so I disconnected it to try and clean it out. Just as I got the hose disconnected, Deacon Tom came up behind me and shouted, "What are you doing?!'

Meg nodded and leaned forward, signaling him to continue.

"I'm sure he shouted so I could hear him over all the racket, but he startled me. I didn't even know he was there. I didn't hear him come into the boiler room. I jumped. I had a flashback to when my squad was ambushed in Afghanistan. I had a wrench in my hand. I lashed out and swung the wrench. He was stooping down, and it caught him on the back of the head. He fell to the floor. I don't remember anything after that. I just panicked and ran. I don't even know where I went. I don't remember anything further until at some point I found myself in the church, and I heard sirens, I saw the kids filing into the church and I saw the fire engines pulling into the driveway."

He looked at the wall for a few minutes, then took a breath and continued.

"I didn't know he was dead. When I found out, I was devastated. I was terrified. I didn't say anything because I was so scared. What could I say? Nobody would believe such a crazy story."

Meg leaned back. "That's where you're wrong, Bob. I believe you. This is pretty much what I had already worked out. I just didn't know the details, but I knew that something like this had to be what happened. Nothing else made any sense."

"Does anybody else know?" he asked.

"My superiors know. The District Attorney knows. We all agreed that I would meet with you to see if you could help us with the details."

"What's going to happen to me now?" he demanded.

"I don't know exactly," Meg said. "It's up to the District Attorney. But we're going to get you some help. Everything is going to be alright, Bob. This is definitely not a murder case any longer. You didn't mean to kill Deacon Tom. There is no criminal intent here. I'm going to leave you for a few minutes and confer with the brass. I'll have another officer come in and sit with you and keep you company, offer you some coffee or tea. I won't be gone long, then I'll come back and we'll talk about what happens next. You've been very helpful to us Bob. We'll do everything we can to help you, too."

Glinski just nodded and resumed examining the carpet. "Thank you for understanding, Meg," he said.

Meg left the interview room, and walked into the adjacent room behind the one-way mirror. D.A. Farley, Inspector Flanagan and Joe were all seated behind the glass.

"Great job, Meg," Flanagan said.

"Superb. Very professional," Farley said. "I don't mind telling you it's a great relief to have this case solved. The community and the press have been up in arms."

"Nice job, Meg," Joe agreed. His eyes sparkled with pride that went way beyond his careful, professional response.

"Thank you. I was very nervous. What happens now?" Meg asked.

All eyes turned to Farley.

"Clearly, this is not a murder case. I don't think it's even a manslaughter case. There's no criminal intent. It appears that he wasn't aware of what he was doing, and that he acted under what the law calls an "extreme emotional disturbance."

"We'll take him before a judge on some minor charge just to hold him temporarily, and we'll get the judge to order a forensic mental health examination under Article 730 of the Criminal Procedure Law. He'll be examined by two psychiatrists from the County Forensic Mental Health Service. I'm confident that they will say that he was mentally impaired and not responsible for his actions at the time."

"Then what will happen to him?" Meg asked.

"It will be out of our hands at that point," Farley said, "but he won't go to trial or to prison. The Department of Mental Hygiene will work out a treatment plan for him. Good job, everyone. I'll take care of it from here."

CHAPTER 25

THE NEXT FEW DAYS WERE A WHIRLWIND of activity, but later on it all melted into a sort of a blur in Meg's memory. Bob Glinski was assigned an attorney by the Assigned Counsel Program of the Bar Association. He was taken before a judge and arraigned on a minor charge of tampering with evidence, mainly to give the court jurisdiction. The D.A.'s Office requested a forensic mental health examination. Glinski's attorney did not object, and he was sent to the County Medical Center to be examined by two consulting psychiatrists, who would write reports giving the court their expert opinion of his mental status.

D.A. Farley presented the case to a County Grand Jury, mainly to cover his own flank. But when he informed the Grand Jury that his office was unable to allege that Glinski posessed the requisite *mens rea* (criminal intent) to commit the murder or even manslaughter, the jury declined to vote an indictment.

Meg, Joe and Inspector Flanagan were given the unenviable task of meeting with Father Vince and Deacon Tom's wife Sheila, and explaining to them that the case was solved, but that nobody was going to be charged or indicted. They were all dreading the meeting. They expected Father Vince and Tom's wife to be angry and outraged that nobody was going to be prosecuted for Tom's death. The meeting, having been arranged through Father Vince, took place in Sheila's living room. She served everyone tea and Irish soda bread. The Inspector began by announcing that the police had solved the case. After some preliminaries, he turned it over to Meg to handle the narrative. She gently and painstakingly went through the steps of the investigation, ending with the conclusion that the death had been accidental and that Glinski was not mentally culpable. Meg, Joe and the Flannagan held their breath, expecting outrage and protest. But, to their surprise, both Sheila and Father Vince took the news calmly and with understanding. They both quite realized that Bob Glinski was not in his right mind, and did not intend to hurt Tom.

In due course the two consulting psychiatrists issued their report, finding that Bob Glinski was suffering from PTSD, with secondary diagnoses of depression and anxiety disorder, and that he was not acting responsibly or with intent at the time of the incident. Glinski was sent to a mental hospital for extended treatment.

St. Brendan's parish slowly returned to normal. Father Vince brought in a financial consultant who improved tuition collection procedures enormously, and also introduced some fundraising efforts which brought in significantly more money. It seemed that, awakened from their lethargy by the tragedy, everyone pulled together and did more to help. In a short time, the school and the parish were on a sound footing again. One of the fundraising efforts was a $100-a-plate dinner to establish a scholarship fund in honor of Deacon Tom. It was attended by more than 300 people, and, with the sale of program ads and sponsorship, it raised more than $40,000 for the scholarship fund.

Meg and Joe continued to date regularly and exclusively, becoming a well-known item in A District and in the Department. Meg returned to uniform duty, driving a black and white up and down the streets of the South Side. But not for long. One afternoon, while on patrol, she received a radio message to report to the Commissioner's Office.

'Oh gosh, what did I do now?' she thought. 'Somebody probably reported me for meeting Joe so many times for coffee while on duty.'

When she reached Headquarters, she took the elevator to the third floor and entered the Commissioner's suite. "Go right in," the receptionist said. "The Commissioner is waiting for you." She swallowed hard and entered the office. She was startled to see Inspector Flanagan, Joe, and Father Vince, all having coffee with the Commissioner.

She knew that something was up, but she couldn't figure out what. She thought maybe she had screwed something up.

"It's about time you got here," the Commissioner said. "Come here." She approached, and he opened his desk drawer and took out a leather case and presented it to her.

"Open it up," he commanded. She opened the case. It contained a gold detective's badge.

"You made it. You've proven yourself. Your father is looking down from heaven with pride today," he said with a smile..

"You will be assigned to A District detectives, starting tomorrow. Since you worked so well on this case with a guy named Joe Curran, he will be your partner. He'll show you the ropes, and probably teach you all his bad habits as well."

Meg started to tear up. Father Vince's mouth was twitching. Joe seemed to have something in his eye that he was rubbing furiously. Inspector Flanagan had something caught in his throat. There was much hand-shaking and back-slapping.

Then there were smiles and hugs all the way around, handshakes and a few kisses as well.

"Take the rest of the shift off," the Commissioner said. "I'm sure that, ah, you and your new partner have some celebrating to do tonight.

And that's the story of how Meg Ryan got her gold badge.

Epilogue

MEG RYAN AND JOE CURRY CONTINUED
to work on solving crimes in A District, and continued
to date, growing to know each other more and more and
be comfortable with each other. They were together, on
and off the job. Joe was learning how to make linguine
carbonara. Thee went to church together on Sunday,
alternating between St. Brendan's and St. Anthony's,
between the English Mass and the Latin Mass. The
parish started to pull together more than it ever had,
and the school was restored to fiscal health. Meg cor-
responded by letter (not email, but real old-fashioned
letters) with Bob Glinski, who was receiving indefinite
treatment at Marcy State Hospital, a division of the
State Department of Mental Hygiene.

One day, about six months later, Meg decided to
visit Bob at Marcy. She took a personal leave day from
work, and drove to the hospital, which was about a
three-hour drive from the city. As she was walking up

to the front entrance of the hospital, she was shocked to see Sheila Flynn coming out of the front door. They both stopped and stared at each other.

"Sheila, what are you doing here?" Meg asked in surprise after giving Sheila a big hug and a kiss on the cheek.

"I was visiting Bob Glinski. I take him communion once a week," the older woman answered.

"I'm amazed. I didn't know that," Meg said.

"Well, I just felt compelled to do it. I felt like it's the kind of thing that Tom would want me to do," she said. "What are you doing here?"

"I came to visit Bob as well, but in my case it's the first time since he's been in here. How is he doing?"

"Very well," Sheila said. "I think he's found peace. You will be surprised when you see him."

They chatted for a few more minutes, and then said goodbye. Sheila walked to her car and Meg entered the facility, showed her badge, and explained that she had made arrangements for a visit with Bob Glinski.

"Yes, we were expecting you," the attendant said. She was taken a meeting room, furnished like a living room, with several armchairs, some end tables, a coffee table, some paintings on the pale green walls, and some fresh flowers on the coffee table. She looked at the paintings on the wall, mostly landscapes, probably done by patients, she guessed. The door opened and Bob entered the room. He was dressed in a polo shirt and khaki slacks.

They stood there looking at each other awkwardly. Then she held out her hands and took both his hands in hers and stood back.

"Hello, Bob. It's good to see you. You look healthier than I've ever seen you before."

"Thanks for coming, Meg," he said. "Yes, my medication is better adjusted, and I'm getting counseling and group therapy every day, and I do feel a lot better."

They sat down in two of the armchairs and began to chat. Meg brought Bob up to date on all of the happenings in the parish.

Bob mentioned that in addition to Sheila, Father Vince comes to see him twice a month.

"How do you spend you days, Bob," Meg asked.

"Well, apart from counseling and group therapy, I spend most of my time in the art room. I've discovered that I can draw and paint. They have a really good art teacher here, and I really enjoy it. It relaxes me, and gives me a sense of accomplishment."

"Really? That's very interesting," she said.

"Would you like to see some of my work?" he asked eagerly.

"Yes, I'd love to," she answered.

"Then follow me," he said. He led her down the hall and around a few corners to an art studio. There were easels with canvasses in various stages of completion on them, tables with sketching pads on them, and paint brushes, palates and cloths scattered around the room, in the typical disarray of a well used art studio.

"Here is some of my work over here,' he said, guiding her to the far side of the room. There was a blackboard on the wall, and on the chalk tray under the blackboard, various paintings—oil on canvas, were standing up. He pointed to one of the works, an oil painting depicting the familiar scene of the Agony in the Garden, with Jesus kneeling by large rock praying, and Peter and some of the other apostles asleep on the ground at various places around him.

"Is this your work, Bob?" she asked.

"Yes," he said. That is the first oil I did. This one over here is also one of mine," he said as he pointed out a painting of the Crowning With Thorns.

Meg stepped back and regarded both paintings at some length.

"Those are really quite good," she exclaimed. "Had you ever done art before?" she asked.

"Never," he said. "I didn't think I could draw at all, but they have a great art teacher here. She really draws out the talent in people.

"This is wonderful, Bob," she gushed. "It's amazing. You have quite a talent."

She paused for a minute, and looked at him.

"I have an idea," she said. "St. Michael the Archangel is the patron of police officers. Do you think you could do a painting of St. Michael the archangel that we could hang in the Detectives Squad Room? You can find dozens of portrayals of him on the internet. Of course, as an angel, he's pure spirit, so he doesn't have a body, but he's always depicted in art as a knight in shining armor, with a spear in his hand, casting Satan out of paradise. Do you think you could find one of those images on the internet and do an oil painting of it?"

His face lit up. "Yes, as long as I can find an image to work from, I'm sure I could do it."

"Good. Just Google St. Michael the Archangel. You can find anything on Google these days. You'll come up with dozens of artists rendering of St. Michael, but they all look pretty much the same. He'll look like a medieval knight in shining armor, carrying a spear and vanquishing the devil."

"I'll get on it right away," Bob said.

"How long do you think it will take?" Meg asked.

"Give me a couple of weeks. I'll make it my priority."

"Good," she said. "Let me know when it's done, and I'll come and collect it."

Meg stayed another half-hour, and they said many things to each other. When she left, they each felt like they had found a new friend.

9 781545 674826